CW00347761

There was ⟨a ⟩
in his house⟨ ⟩

Dan ascended t⟨ ⟩
only his penlig⟨ht ⟩
bedrooms in al⟨l ⟩

Everything was undisturbed.

Except his private bathroom. As Dan surveyed the room, a mound of clothing caught his eye. His bold visitor had arrived in a cellophane drugstore raincoat. A white denim sunsuit cut high on the hip. Sheer nylon panties cut even higher on the hip. T-shirt and anklets in a matching shade of mint green. And lastly, a pair of cookie-crumb-covered sneakers.

His steel-trap mind devised a composite sketch of his intruder. A pint-size blonde sugar junkie.

Discomfort and Joy!

Dan raced back to his bedroom for a closer look. This time his penlight picked her up, cuddled in the window seat, sound asleep. It was a trap, and he'd walked right into it!

Dear Reader

What better way to brighten up the long, dark winter months than by reading an exciting Temptation novel, especially when Temptation has caught the festive spirit with its bright new raspberry-coloured covers.

This will be our new look for 1995—the year when Temptation gets to celebrate its 10th Anniversary!—so step into Christmas and the New Year with even more passionate, fun-loving stories from Temptation. We know you'll enjoy the good reading we have lined up for you in the year ahead.

The Editor
Mills & Boon Temptation
Eton House
18-24 Paradise Road
Richmond
Surrey TW9 1SR

Joyride

LEANDRA LOGAN

MILLS & BOON LIMITED
ETON HOUSE, 18-24 PARADISE ROAD
RICHMOND, SURREY TW9 1SR

MILLS & BOON and the Rose Device are trademarks of the
publisher. TEMPTATION is a trademark of Harlequin Enterprises
Limited, used under licence.

First published in Great Britain in 1994
by Mills & Boon Limited, Eton House, 18-24 Paradise Road,
Richmond, Surrey TW9 1SR

© Mary Schultz 1993

ISBN 0 263 79006 1

21 - 9412

Printed in Great Britain by
BPC Paperbacks Ltd

Prologue

Blue Christmas Past

"I'M A FREE WOMAN, Danny!" Joy Jones cried out in relief. "It's all over!"

It wasn't over by a long shot.

Detective Dan Burke, a dark solid figure in his snow-dusted topcoat, stood stock-still in the center of the downtown St. Paul hotel room they'd shared during the trial. They'd packed their suitcases this morning, anticipating today's "guilty" verdict. Now, as dusk fell over the city, he wasn't certain of Joy's fate.

Regarding her from the shelter of a hooded gaze, he sifted through his explanations—ones of gravity and sensibility, ones that should come naturally. His fellow police officers were accustomed to his inscrutable expression, his serious outlook on life in general. It had earned him the nickname By-the-Book Burke around the police department. Only Joy had never accepted his hard shell at face value.

Dan still couldn't believe that Joy had found his secret buttons, and had the nerve to push them over and over again. During their eight weeks together in captivity—first in a department-owned safe house, then in this hotel—she'd taken delight in kicking down all his emotional fences, tugging loose his playful side.

Protecting her had been his pleasure. Pleasing her was now an obsession—one they unfortunately could no longer afford. He had to call the shots this one last time without any regard to her feelings. Life couldn't get any tougher.

"Free as air . . ." Joy lilted whimsically.

She was whirling and swaying around the room, peeling off the conservative brown suit they'd purchased to enhance her credibility on the witness stand. Joy was a blond nymph of ninety pounds, a footloose spirit who had little time for the rules Dan revered, and a woman who thought nothing of dropping the offending tailored jacket and skirt into the wastebasket.

She was the most captivating creature he'd ever encountered in all his thirty years.

Against his better judgment, Dan was beginning to let the headiness of her movements take him in. She was down to her slip, the beige crepe blouse having joined the collection in the trash. The bra would go next. Dan squeezed his eyes shut, hoping to quell his humming nerves.

Dangerous curves ahead.

He'd been down this road often enough to know the signs. Joy was temptation. His first slipup on duty. Dan had been the ultimate bodyguard. He'd served, he'd protected. And he'd tasted.

Even now, in retrospect, he couldn't imagine resisting her. Their torrid affair had been the highlight of his life. A supercharged joyride like he'd never fantasized about even in his youth.

But would she also be his ultimate downfall?

Every Minnesotan with a television or a newspaper knew Joy Jones as the Kodak Comic, the star witness of the Jerome Berkley murder trial. Berkley, a police lieutenant for the city of St. Paul, claimed he was out on the town the night his wife was brutally murdered in their home. At the time of the attack he claimed to be at the Laff Trak Comedy Club, enjoying the stage act in the private booth of club owner Theo Nelson.

Joy, a local comedienne headlining at the Laff Trak, had blown Jerome Berkley's alibi to bits when she reported that Berkley had not been there that night at all. Her photographic memory—and the conservative suit—had made her a most credible witness. Only hours ago Berkley was convicted of murdering his wife.

Dan had been so proud of Joy, risking her life to set the record straight. The case was an ugly one, crossing into the gray areas of loyalties and personalities—Berkley was a cop in Dan's department, and Theo Nelson was an old pal of Joy's.

Learning that the Laff Trak was a meeting place for lowlifes as well as a money-laundering operation, had broken Joy's heart. The last thing Dan wanted was to break it for a second time. But keeping her alive was his job. First and foremost, Dan was a realistic cop. And Joy wasn't the free woman she wanted to be.

She turned on the radio and a Christmas melody filled the impersonal suite with a surprisingly homey feeling. Joy looked so sweet, so relaxed as she swayed to the music in her scanty lace slip, her luxuriant blond hair a sweeping curtain on her bare shoulders.

During the dark, dreary nights at the secluded safe house she'd been like a frightened child-woman, fending off the depression so commonly associated with isolation. The snap of a branch or the bark of a dog had set them both off. Full of sweetness and spontaneity, she'd seeped into his every pore like warm liqueur. Dan had eagerly participated in her tantalizing games of seduction, confident all the while that they were both consenting adults indulging their innermost fantasies. In an especially dizzying moment of abandon he'd promised her a cozy Christmas at his house after the trial. She'd really liked that idea. It soon became the focal point of many an afterglow moment, forcing Dan to embellish outlandishly on the festivities. Now, it seemed, his lies wouldn't matter.

"Don't go near the window, Joy!"

Joy whirled at his sharp-edged command, her hand still on the hem of the drape. "It's all right. We're on the fifteenth floor. No one's going to see me in my underwear. Not unless they're in the high rise across the street spying on me with a telescope."

Or a high-powered rifle.

"Please back away," he reiterated in low, deliberate tones.

Joy obeyed, as she had all his official directions. But she was puzzled. "I only wanted to see if it was still snowing."

Dan exhaled as she sauntered toward him. "Come over here, to the bed."

"Always the rascal beneath that shiny badge, aren't you?" With a playful purr she wound her arms around his starched white collar, digging her toe into his sock. A full foot shorter than he, she had to pull him down to capture his mouth.

Dan kissed her back with passion, with greed. Her tongue was like a flame in his mouth. As with all her overtures, Dan was instantly aroused. He'd never responded so swiftly and completely to any other woman. Her powers were frightening and exhilarating at the same time.

Joy was working on his clothing now. The heavy woolen coat dropped off his back, shirt buttons popped beneath his knotted silk tie, and his trousers rustled down the length of his legs to the toes of his polished leather shoes. Arching her small body against his, Joy urged him on, running the pads of her fingers over the sensitive backs of his thighs.

Blood pounded in his temples. Longing burned in his belly. But an inner voice of reason—a voice that had been quelled far too often by this seductress—reminded him that this mustn't happen. Mustering his last ounce of self-control he reached back to pry her hands from him, halting her backward march to the mattress.

"We gotta talk, honey."

"After—"

"Now."

Dan's breath was heaving and labored as he squeezed her fingers in his and guided them to his chest. They were so small. She was so small. If only he could slip her into his pocket for a year. Pluck her out safe and sound next Christmas.

"It is over, isn't it?" Her soft, thick voice held a trace of doubt, as did her vivid green eyes.

"Not exactly," he said gently. "Not as we planned."

"But you promised!" she lashed back in fury, breaking free of his grasp. "I cooperated, I testified. Now I should be free!"

Joy's artistic temperament was fragile in a way that totally baffled Dan. Her emotions swam just beneath a layer of hip bravado, surfacing with the slightest jar.

She was the type of woman who cried over sentimental commercials, who objected vehemently if someone cut in front of her in a checkout line. A baffling woman. A terrifying woman! The way she drew on his own buried sensitivities was a crime in itself!

"Please listen, Joy."

Joy icily stared him down from the opposite side of the room.

Dan felt the arctic chill to the very core of his heart. Stone-cold and stark-naked. Suddenly aware of his vulnerable state of dress, he yanked up his pants.

"I'm afraid we may be sitting ducks in this hotel room," he declared in level tones even though his heart was breaking. The reserve he'd nurtured since childhood served him well.

"We've been here a week! And out at that farmhouse a whole lot longer. Why now, copper?"

"I figure it's because the jury ultimately believed your story and found Jerome Berkley guilty. Perhaps certain factions didn't taken you seriously until now. Until tonight."

Her lower lip trembled. "What makes you think so?"

"That call I got at the courthouse. It was from a guy known only to me as Repeat. He's a reliable informant—"

"A paid tipster, you mean," she blurted back with surprising conviction.

"An informant," he maintained, buttoning his shirt, "who has frequently provided me with pertinent information."

Joy tossed her head with a noise of disgust. "A hired snitch who would eavesdrop on his own grandmother for a buck. Who barhops his way between St. Paul and

Minneapolis." Arms folded across the bodice of her slip, Joy eyed him belligerently. "After six years of working nightclubs around the Twin Cities, I know the score."

Dan drew a sharp breath. "How can you condemn him when you don't even know what he had to say?"

"Because it was about me, you dummy!" she cried out brokenly. "Because I don't want any more trouble."

As Joy turned her back, Dan realized he'd been a fool to think he could remain the complete professional. He closed the space between them and hugged her hard.

"I know it's been tough, honey," he rasped as she buried her face in his snowy white shirt. "With Theo's fall and all."

When Joy had originally come to the police station and told Dan her story about Berkley, she hadn't realized just what damage her knowledge would ultimately do to her boss and friend, Theo Nelson. She'd known Theo wasn't choirboy clean, but she'd never dreamed that the Laff Trak was a money-laundering outlet. Jerome Berkley was the mastermind, but Theo had ended up in a lot of trouble for his part in it. Watching him sink had devastated Joy. Theo had wisely turned state's evidence, recanting his original statement about Berkley being in the club the night of his wife's death. In a plea bargain, he ended up with a two-year sentence.

She lifted her eyes with a sniffle. "Guess I'm ready. Let me have it."

"According to Repeat, there are still a couple of bad cops floating around the Twin Cities. Ones who feel you could incriminate them."

She stomped her foot on the plush carpet. "But I can't! I told you everything I know."

"It's your photographic memory they're afraid of. They fear that something will click and you'll remember seeing them at the club, link them to an illegal act."

"Just because I remember that Lieutenant Berkley wasn't seated in Theo's private booth the night of his wife's murder, doesn't mean that I can flip back through each and every night I worked."

"I know it." Dan cupped her chin in his hand and massaged her tender skin with his thumb. "But you did recall specific dates when Berkley was at the club, and you did witness an envelope bulging with money being passed from Berkley to Theo the week before the murder. No doubt a bribe for Theo's false alibi."

"But the envelope was never recovered! And Theo denies getting a cent."

"Fortunately, we got a conviction anyway. But your talent for detail has obviously been noted by a couple of Berkley's henchmen who are still on the loose."

"I can only remember the things I pay attention to," Joy objected in exasperation. "I noticed Berkley on and off because he is a very attractive man. And the night of Mrs. Berkley's murder stuck out in my mind because Theo was entertaining a couple of very tacky ladies who were all over him like cheap perfume. Ladies that Berkley wouldn't have given the time of day."

"Yes, and having those very tacky ladies tracked down was a wonderful addition to our case," he consoled gently.

"So send the word back through this Repeat," she ordered with a poke to his chest. "I can't hurt anybody. I just want to go on with my life."

"It isn't that simple, Joy. The good guys and the bad guys are all wearing gray hats. I don't know who I can trust on the force right now."

Joy blinked, her eyes steady on his. "What are you telling me?"

"You're going to need protection for a while longer," he said.

"I'll hide in the basement of that wonderful old mansion of yours," she proposed in a rush of panic. "Then we can still have our spectacular Christmas. The one you guaranteed."

"No, Joy. I've already made some arrangements for you through the Feds. Considering that the laundering operation overlapped in their jurisdiction, they were more than happy to oblige."

Joy tensed in his arms. "Do you mean what I think you mean?"

Dan nodded soberly. "The federal Witness Protection Program. Believe me, it's the only way I can ensure your safety."

"But I've already given up so much."

"For a worthy end you can be proud of," Dan said.

"Doing my civic duty shouldn't be costing me so much," she lamented. "I've already lost my friendship with Theo, my job at his club. I've even lost the trust of some of my fellow performers and fans. Some of them think I made up the part about seeing the envelope of money pass between Theo and Jerome Berkley just to get more recognition." She fumed in disgust. "I wouldn't have deliberately hurt Theo with a lie."

Dan grimaced. He didn't share Joy's sentimentality for Theo Nelson. The creep had taken Joy hostage when the police had stormed the Laff Trak to arrest him after

Joy's show one night. The bumbling idiot had never learned to drive, and in desperation had commandeered Joy and her car. With a gun in one hand and Joy's statue of the patron saint of travel, Saint Christopher, in the other, Theo had forced Joy into a high-speed chase with the police.

"You're saying goodbye, aren't you, copper?"

The question was posed with a spring of fresh tears, confusing and disconcerting him. Surely she wasn't expecting any sort of future with him! No, of course not. She was just overreacting, as she always did. Though emotional, Joy was intelligent. Surely she could see just as well as he that they were totally incompatible. Joy lived in the fast-paced club scene. Shone at night and slept till noon. Dan worked the day shift and used his evenings for relaxation.

Still, he'd miss the incredible sex. But they couldn't live between the sheets and she would eventually find his personal routine dull. And that would really hurt. Besides, he'd always envisioned himself committing to a woman he could understand outside the bedroom.

"And I won't allow the system to swallow me up," Joy was proclaiming as he plugged back into the present moment. "They won't be taking away my precious identity along with everything else."

"Joy, I will know exactly who you are and where you are the entire time. If something major breaks, I will come for you immediately."

"That could take forever!"

"I'm pretty good at my job," he retorted defensively.

"Think you can fix things before Christmas?" she asked.

"In five lousy days?"

"You promised me it would be all right by then. I trusted you."

"The very fact that you are still alive and arguing should tell you something about my skills," he countered heatedly.

"I couldn't feel a bit alive with my act, my name, my freedom all stripped away from me," she said with a proud lift of her chin.

"Of course, you could," he consoled. "I promise you it will only be temporary."

Joy raised her clenched fists in the air as if primed for a boxing match. "Don't you dare make me any more promises, mister! Don't you dare!"

Dan had just gotten a good grip on her wrists when the telephone rang. With a sudden swing he dropped her to the mattress. "Keep very quiet. It could be one of those gray hats I was talking about." Once satisfied that her pursed lips were going to stay closed, he picked up the receiver.

"Oh, it's you. Yes, we're set on this end. . . ." Dan swiftly clamped his free hand over her mouth to quell her gasp of indignation. "Great. Five minutes."

"I've never heard so many yeses come out of you at one time," she huffed upon release, rolling out of reach on the huge mattress.

"The hell you haven't."

"So, when is my sentence supposed to start, gov'na?" Joy cackled in a high voice, setting her features in a cronelike distortion.

Dan knew it was her job, taking on other personalities with the flip of an internal switch; but it hurt that she would turn on him so completely. All along, he'd had her trust. When all the other authority figures from all the other agencies had been a dismal blur, he'd been her sterling knight.

"Don't move a muscle while I'm gone," he directed, easing off the bed. He retrieved his coat from the carpet where Joy had tossed it and headed for the door. "And get your suit back on."

"You're contradicting yourself," she sassed, hurling a pillow at him.

He caught it in midair and tossed it back. "Knock it off. I want you dressed and ready when I get back with your papers. It'll be fifteen minutes or so."

"Danny?" she called after him softly.

He gripped the doorknob, a lump in his throat the size of a grapefruit. "Yeah, honey?"

"How can something that feels so wrong be good for me?"

Dan's analytical mind couldn't compute the question. The idea of acting on one's feelings in a situation like this was beyond comprehension. "Joy, logic and experience tell me that this is the only way."

"About Christmas," she called out as he gripped the knob.

She was stalling. Only children put this much stock in Christmas. Hell, she was twenty-five years old. He shot her a last look full of strain and urgency. "Your safety is what matters right now. One lost Christmas isn't that much of a sacrifice."

"You know what you are, Dan Burke. A control freak, that's what! You toyed with my life and now you're throwing me away!"

Dan let the words bounce off his back, not able to face the harsh message. "If you care about your life half as much as I do, you'll grow up and follow orders."

It didn't occur to him, not for a single second, that she'd disobey him. So when he came back to the empty hotel room and found her note, he felt like a major chump. Her message was short and to the point: She couldn't sacrifice her total identity for the promise of safety—she had to be free to live.

Numbly he searched the room for any clue to her destination—an indentation on a notepad, a page open in the phone book—all the while taking silent inventory of exactly what was missing.

He could do without the little things she stole: junk food, pocket change, the old Metro Police sweatshirt. It wasn't until much later that night, after he'd frantically searched the Twin Cities for her to no avail, that he discovered just what else she'd taken: his heart. She'd stolen it away piece by piece, right out from under his nose.

1

Nobody oughtta be alone...

"JOY TO THE WORLD!"

Joy Jones, alias Faye Fairway, froze in her tracks on the sidewalk outside her Orlando apartment house. Tides of emotion, as strong as those of the nearby Atlantic, washed over her in blanketing comfort. It had been a whole year since she'd heard her real name called out in greeting. How touching that it was on the lips of her jovial landlord, Henry Sheldon.

Joy...

Intent on savoring the moment, she remained near the busy street, watching Henry position a huge mechanical Santa Claus on the small square of grass fronting the four-story brick building. The doll's red velvet jacket was hanging open and a door in its barrel-shaped belly was pulled back to expose a mass of color-coded wires—certainly the nuts and bolts of Christmas in its barest form. But the opportunity for a pure, sweet Yuletide was all Joy could see—and hear. She was unable to resist asking him to repeat himself.

The stout curmudgeon in his baggy dungarees and plaid short-sleeved shirt shook his screwdriver, his round, aged face alight. "I was just sayin', 'Joy to the world!'"

A simple pleasure in her very complicated life. It wouldn't hurt to pretend for a moment, would it? Pretend that this warm man she'd known for two short months was really calling her Joy? The heavy grocery bag in her arms seemed feather light as she indulged herself, slipping into her real identity to see if it still fit. For just a precious moment she was not the fictional Faye Fairway, part-time server at the coffee shop down the street. She was once again Joy Jones, the wildly creative comedienne from Minnesota, with a flair for humor and poignancy; for making 'em laugh till they cried and cry till they laughed.

Joy had been living on the run for twelve months, switching personas as frequently as most women switched lipstick. Fleeing from unknown enemies and a cogent broken heart, she'd taken her professional stand-up act on the road, portraying one, then another of the eccentric characters from her stage act.

Her disguises proved to be as believable in everyday life as they were under the footlights, for they were all well-rounded women she'd created with loving care. But there was always that fine line between Joy and her creations. Though she could only leave the "stage" behind closed doors, she was always Joy deep inside—no matter what the outside wrapping reflected.

"Get over here, Faye, and give me your opinion!" Henry bellowed heartily.

Faye Fairway fit in nicely with the other tenants at the Tropical Arms Apartments. She was Joy's last invention, the character she'd been putting together right before the Berkley trial—a spicy career waitress with hair the color of red-hot pepper and a hip that when cocked just so, could balance a tray of home-style dinners complete with condiments. Portraying Faye at this point was a downright necessity. Joy's savings were depleted and she needed a new cash flow. Some of her other characters—such as the retired princess from the small mythical country of Dubinspan, and the dippy blond weather girl—weren't as easy to hire out. But waitressing was always a good employment bet. It was the third time she'd used Faye.

Inhaling a fortifying breath of ocean-tinged air, she cut across the grass, anxious to go inside and remove her hot wig. It was generating kiln-intensity heat right down to the roots of her very blond hair.

"So, what do you think of my plump plastic fellow?" Henry Sheldon peeled off his tan fisherman's hat and wiped his sweaty brow with a hankie, casually looking skyward.

Joy knew that behind his calm gaze he was dying for her gush of approval. She nodded at the ten-foot robot standing stout and jolly between twin flowering shrubs. "He's magnificent! And you set him up so quickly, during my short trip to the market."

"Yep, yep." He planted his hands on his doughy waistline, his round face aglow. "Won't the missus be surprised when she gets back from her Tampa trip tonight. Every year I tell her that old Santy is too much bother. Every year she coaxes the kiddies up and down the street to ask for his reappearance. I always surrender in the end."

"I hear you make a pretty good Santa yourself, at the annual Christmas Eve party here at the Arms."

"I do keep ahoppin' right through New Year's," he conceded.

"Loving every minute of it," Joy accused with a grin.

"I love teasing the missus the most," he told her with a wink.

"Humor is the key to a long-lasting relationship."

Henry's face lit up tenderly. "It's hard to believe you haven't been snatched up by a young fella yet."

Joy shrugged as betraying visions of Dan Burke danced in her head. She'd been snatched up, all right. Then smacked back down in rejection. The regulation nut just hadn't understood her freestyle spirit. A whole year of pondering their dynamite attraction had left her wondering just how it ever happened in the first place. Had there been anything cerebral beneath all that stupendous hot sex? Oh, how she wanted to find out!

Joy tugged at her wig, blaming her naughty thoughts on its pressure-cooker fit. It had been a pitifully long, celibate year.

"Guess I've been on the move far too much lately to make any real ties," she murmured evasively, digging the toe of her tennis shoe into the grass.

"Well, we're more than delighted that you found your way to our doorstep," he assured her. "And kind . . . Why, the way you lent the missus your car for her excursion to her sister's. The stick shift in our Jeep makes her nervous on long hauls, and your Plymouth was a lifesaver."

Joy beamed under his praise. "I was glad to help out."

"It's your nature, pure and simple. And some nice young man will come along and spot your attributes. You're still young. Plenty of time to mend that broken heart of yours."

Joy cringed sheepishly. "You noticed?"

"Can't miss it, tacked to your sleeve."

Obviously her act needed some work!

"Even the approaching holidays have barely brought a glimmer of real joy to your disposition."

A glimmer of real Joy. How accidentally prophetic.

"I imagine you're accustomed to snowy winters, being a Midwesterner and all."

She'd obviously been talking too much, revealing bits and pieces about her real past. But Henry and the other friendly tenants were just too hard to resist.

"Well, the spirit of the season is all in one's attitude," he sermonized with open pleasure. "These laurustinus plants here are a Christmas tree of sorts, if you wish to see them that way." He gestured to the greenery flanking Santa. "They're strong enough to flower in winter, and the blossoms are white, as though they're dappled with snow."

"They are lovely," she conceded, shifting her grocery bag from one arm to the other. "But to be perfectly honest, I've always felt that Christmas only magnifies the loneliness of those who are alone."

"But you're not alone, Faye! For one thing, you've got all of us here at the Tropical Arms. We're a blended family. Always room for one more."

Music to her ears. So much so, that she didn't pick up on the crafty lilt in his tone. Joy so wanted to count on their hospitality for the holidays. Of course, it wouldn't be as grand as the Christmas she'd almost spent with Dan at his ancestral home in St. Paul. If Dan didn't answer the forgive-and-forget card she'd sent him with her current address, here she would stay—at least through the New Year.

She patted her steamy head. A homey Christmas in ninety-degree weather. Who'd ever have guessed it of a Minnesota snow bunny?

Joy watched as Henry peeled off his hat and dropped to his knees before the mechanical Santa. He poked his screwdriver into the open belly, rattled it around, and then requested his pliers. Joy leaped into action, setting her groceries against a potted plant on the stoop, rooting out the pliers from Henry's toolbox on the lawn. Henry gripped the tool then dipped his head clean inside the hollow doll.

"Hold 'em steady," his voice echoed. "Very delicate work here, my girl."

Joy circled behind Henry and took ahold of the doll's torso from the side. The white furry collar of the jacket tickled her nose, but she suppressed a sneeze in honor of the cause.

Maybe Dan would answer the card. There was still time. Six days.

What if he was so furious over her flight that he'd written her off for good? At the very least, she'd like to know if the danger had passed. So she could go home and start anew. He'd respond, she consoled herself, even if only officially. Duty was the number-one priority in Dan Burke's life.

"Got a wire tangled up in the armpit," Henry reported through the hollow figure.

As he shifted, Santa teetered in Joy's grip. She hugged it hard. Her move caused its velvet pants to drop, plastic black belt and all. Looking at the britches pooled on the figure's shoes, she didn't know whether to laugh or cry. It was Dan's dilemma at the hotel all over again. That was how she chose to remember him: vulnerable, masculine, sexy and silly with his fancy trousers at his feet.

"What the heck . . ." Henry bobbed out for air, his round face set in bemusement. "Feels like an earthquake in there!"

"Sorry. Lost my grip." Tears were rolling down Joy's cheeks as she laughed in breathless gasps, her head tipped against Santa's shoulder.

"You all right, Faye?"

"Yeah, sure." Joy sniffed, pulling a tissue from the pocket of her sunsuit.

"I've been meaning to ask you for another favor," he said in hesitation, "but maybe this isn't the right time. . . ."

She dabbed her nose in confusion. "What?"

"Well, I need a new Santa's helper for the do, somebody to dress up with me and help pass out gifts and refreshments. The missus usually does it, but her knees have been giving her trouble."

"I'd love to!" Joy instantly responded, fresh tears springing forth.

"I'm afraid the purse you have forever strapped around your middle won't blend too well with the costume, however," he advised.

Joy gazed down at the black leather fanny pack cinched around her miniscule waist. It didn't harmonize well with today's white denim sunsuit and delicate mint T-shirt, either—or with any of her outfits, for that matter. But she felt compelled to wear it, even over her waitress uniform at the coffee shop. The sack was her security blanket. Full of the necessities for survival, she was prepared for instant flight—if the need arose. It gave her the confidence to move around freely.

Free to flee. The circumstances were certainly ironic. She'd left home to hang on to her identity, but with every stop, she felt it slipping further and further away. But what choice did she have? Assume some identity chosen for her, or live in the shelter of characters that were part of herself? Allow government agents to know her whereabouts and risk a leak, or go off solo with no contact with anyone?

Please, Danny, all I want for Christmas is my old life back.

To Mr. Sheldon she said, "I'll drop the purse for the party."

"Swell." Henry rubbed his meaty palms together in anticipation. "Now, let's give the robot a try. You go plug him in at the outlet behind the bushes and I'll spruce him up."

Henry waited for Joy to return before flipping the switch on the doll's neck. It laboriously hummed to life, its torso twisting in a semicircle, its right arm fanning at the elbow in a wave.

"It's enchanting!" Joy exclaimed in genuine wonder.

"The head glows, too," he boasted, adding a velvet hat as garnishment. "Just needs a new bulb, I'm sure."

Joy circled the doll, tugging the coat into neat folds.

"There just might be one more guest at our dinner table this holiday," Henry ventured suddenly.

Joy shot him a panicky look. He was beaming like an apple-cheeked child with a secret. Joy had once loved secrets. Now the risk factor was too high. "Surely nobody I know," she mumbled.

"Well . . . It seems you haven't been totally up-front about your solitary background," Henry chided.

Joy's body stiffened as though a lightning bolt had sliced through it. Maybe Dan had come for her in answer to her card. "Has someone been here asking for me, Henry?"

"Yes. Your cousin."

That didn't sound like Dan's style. Unless he was trying to protect her cover.

"Said he wanted to surprise you."

Another bad sign. Dan was so darn methodical it was pathetic. And he'd know better than to play games. Joy's green eyes flashed with an intensity that openly startled the landlord. "Tell me what you are talking about, Henry."

"Said his name was Pat Fairway."

"Where did he go? Not to my apartment!"

"No, no, I'd never have let him in your place. I told him right off you weren't home. He said he had some errands to do and would be back."

"But where?" Joy spun toward the street, frantically scanning the traffic and storefronts.

"Can't say for certain." Henry stroked his gray stubbled chin in contemplation. "Just wandered off, I guess. Surely you know this fella?"

Joy shook her head forcefully. Fictional Faye couldn't have a fictional cousin, unless *she* decided as much! "This guy is some kind of imposter."

Henry reared back in surprise. "Well, he sure had the scoop on you. Knows you're slinging hash. Knows your feet are tired out. Knows you miss home. Even wondered if you still drove that old green rattletrap Plymouth. Naturally I thought he was legit. What other explanation could there possibly be?"

The personal stuff had come straight out of the newsy Christmas calling card she'd sent Dan. But Dan wouldn't frighten her this way. "What did you tell him?"

"Nothing, really," he answered, visibly shaken. "Said your car is a Plymouth, but that I'm color-blind. He did seem anxious to continue our talk, but Mrs. Minter in 209 came out to inspect the robot. When I tried to introduce him, he turned and left."

Her car had been green when she fled. For her own protection she'd gotten ahold of some new plates and had the body painted brown. This stalker knew way too much!

"Can you give me a description?" she prompted.

"Not a good one. Tallish, dark hair, brimmed hat, sunglasses. Dressed in a trench coat—in this heat!" He patted the bifocals in his shirt pocket. "I was wearing my reading specs for the intricate work on the wiring. As a matter of fact," he confided uneasily, "I'm not even sure it was a man. Had a strange pitch to his—her—voice."

Her panic grew. "You aren't certain of the gender?"

"It can be borderline," he said defensively. "I have an aunt up in Oregon who can crush a can in her fist and has to shave regular."

Joy shivered in the heat. The disguise was a chilling sign of no good. "This doesn't ring right at all, Henry."

"Just what sort of trouble are you in?" he asked, furrowing his weathered features. "And don't try and tell me different. It's not natural for a young one like you to be drifting, looking over her shoulder all the time."

"I'd like to explain," she intimated softly, "but I don't think we have the time."

"Yes, you'd better go in now," he directed with fatherly noises. "I'll putter around out here until he returns—and put a stop to this nonsense!"

Henry Sheldon and his toolbox were no match for a
rogue cop, or anyone else who might be carrying a
weapon. She had to distance herself quickly.

Joy threw her arms around Henry for a farewell hug.
"I have to go away. At least for a while."

"No, you don't. Let's just go inside and call the police."

Joy wavered. But she wasn't willing to relinquish her
freedom today, any more than she'd been willing to do
so a year ago. "I just can't," she said, stepping backward. "I'll call you. Promise."

"Hey, what about your Christmas?" he protested as
she crossed the lawn.

"Don't worry, Henry," she called back with one last
wave from the sidewalk. "I don't really know what I'm
missing."

2

Better watch out

IT WAS THE DINNER HOUR two days later in St. Paul, Minnesota. Dusk had gathered overhead, enveloping the city in a chilly cloak of purple and gray. Stately Pendham Avenue, nestled miles away from the bustle of downtown, was at its most beautiful. Puffy snowflakes sprinkled over the tall steep rooftops of Pendham's century-old homes and surrounding trees, giving them a pristeen cover. Children dressed in heavy jackets and stocking caps were engaged in a lively broomball game by the glow of the ancient streetlamps, squealing and skidding over the slippery blacktop with robust energy.

The only vehicle in motion on the avenue was a gold sedan. It crawled along with caution, leaving dark ribbons of tread in its wake. St. Paul Police Detective Dan Burke, seated on the passenger side, stared out through the windshield between the gentle slap of the wipers, watching the children, a shouting mass of scrambling shadows. It was like cruising into another dimension, leaving the dirty slush and traffic congestion of the city behind for the old-world tranquility of yesteryear.

"Kids, Christmas and snow!" Rex Cameron's profile lit up with genuine delight behind the wheel of the unmarked police car. "I envy you, buddy, having this

Rockwell scene to roll back into after a day of grueling police work. Quite the cozy setup, if you ask me."

"We're one snug group, all right." Dan deeply regretted the decision to allow his partner to drop him home tonight, rather than vice-versa. Normally Dan let Rex off at his city apartment. But Rex wanted the sedan. His sports coupe was in the shop. There was no way out now. Rex would undoubtedly find out the truth about his status on Pendham once the kids recognized the unmarked police vehicle.

True to his prediction, dramatic war whoops filled the frosty air the instant their headlights pierced the crowd.

"Scrooge!" The players broke apart, darting into the deep front yards for shelter among the oaks and pines, dragging their brooms behind them.

Rex turned to his partner. "You oughtta be ashamed, Danny!"

"It isn't my fault," Dan retorted defensively. "I'm just misunderstood."

Rex pulled up in front of Dan's ancient three-story home. It was a gray-sided, white-shuttered monstrosity dating back to the 1890s. Original features, such as the arched entrance, twin turrets and green shingles remained intact. Dan's colleagues down at the station referred to the place as the Castle.

The Castle, and some of the other Pendham homes, were considered St. Paul landmarks. Dan's father, the late Senator Marcus Burke, had lived his entire life in the house, as had his father before him. The senator and his wife Beth had raised Dan and his older sister Gwen there, as well. Dan liked the stability of staying put.

There were certain things he didn't mess with: daytime law and order, nighttime peace and quiet.

Dan gazed out the passenger window, confident that none of the little mites had bolted onto his land. The Castle's spacious yard was one of the only remaining properties on Pendham still enclosed by the original green spiked fencing. Dan and Floyd Bixley down the way were the last of the ancestral squatters, hanging on to their family homes and cemetery fences for dear life. Though they had little else in common—Dan was thirty and old Floyd was seventy—Dan felt their love of tradition bonded them like blood brothers. Naturally this same attitude kept him apart from the new generation of neighbors who viewed him as a brooding hermit.

And now Rex knew all about it. Dammit anyhow! His partner was always on his case about igniting his social life. Dan was flat certain he'd be dead in a matter of forty-eight hours if he tried to emulate Rex's round-the-clock life-style.

"I thought we were working on our hug-a-cop image out here in wonderland," Rex tsked, shifting into park.

"I can't force people to love me," Dan retorted.

"Have you tried to make contact?" Rex asked mildly.

Dan glowered. "No. Don't want to." He held his breath as Rex scanned the length of the street. All the houses were strung with bright colorful lights, all the front windows displayed full-bodied trees heavy with decoration. Even old Floyd Bixley had a wreath on his front door. Only the Castle remained unadorned.

"You said you'd give it a try this year."

Dan's hawkish profile grew taut. "You know damn well that was last year. Back when I told Joy all those lousy bedtime stories about having merry Christmases around here. When I thought I'd have to make good that pack of lies."

"Well, I still have some of the decorations I picked up for you while you were trapped in the safe house. I could bring them over. Help you spruce things up."

"No, I'm relieved to be halfway off the hook, as it is. We baked those spritz cookies last Saturday with Gwen, and I'll be hosting our annual Christmas reception on Sunday. Then it's all over for me."

"The baking was a lot of fun, Danny. With my family scattered all over the place, I can tell you I really enjoyed it."

Sure, he did. But for Dan the whole brother-sister tradition turned into a fiasco, with his bickering with Gwen about his fling with Joy. Nearly burned a batch of cookies over it!

"Hey, look," Rex suddenly exclaimed, stabbing a finger in the direction of the stucco saltbox across the street. "That little tyke in the blue snowsuit over there has his boot caught in the wire fence surrounding that pine!"

"Timmy Weaver is not stuck. He's a capable six-year-old who likes to pretend that poor fledgling tree is a hairy monster chomping on his toes. It's the highlight of his day to wrestle his boot back to safety," he assured his stunned pal, "and harmless. His mother is watching the whole thing from the side window. See her silhouette?"

"Oh, yeah," Rex noted, craning his neck. "Looks like another wrestler's on the way."

"Jane Weaver. Eight months pregnant and still manages to keep a sharp eye on Timmy. The second she raps on the window to summon him inside, he detours to that poor tree for one last workout."

Rex regarded him dolefully. "How do you know, Scrooge?"

Dan sighed hard, feeling as though his heels were sinking deeper and deeper into quicksand. "Mrs. Nettel, my model neighbor and housekeeper, updates me every Saturday morning while she cleans my cupboards. They're all outside then, you know." Dan groaned in uncharacteristic helplessness. "Running willy-nilly through the yards, whooping like geese, thrashing up snow like puppies. My fence is my only salvation."

"Mrs. Nettel is a liability if she's helping you hide out from the other neighbors."

"You always slant a negative light on her," Dan accused bewilderedly. "She keeps my house neat as a pin and is great company."

Rex shook his head. "I dunno. It's always seemed a little spooky to me, the way she popped up out of nowhere during those first black days of the New Year. Moved in next door and took over your domestic needs almost overnight."

"So what if she dotes?" Dan challenged. "She, too, likes a tight ship."

"I think she hogs your time. Time better divided up between some of the younger, hipper neighbors."

Dan scoped the street, never meeting Rex's interrogative gaze. "I'm no good at chitchat."

"You talk to Mrs. Nettel, don't you?"

"She loves to discuss police work," Dan replied. "And I don't want to hear about how the others have torn out walls and stripped away irreplaceable wood-work."

"You don't know that they've done anything like that," Rex retorted. "Besides, there's nothing wrong with a little change."

Dan frowned at the man behind the wheel, with his salon haircut and green-and-red tie slicing down his shirt. Rex Cameron was a sterling cop and the truest pal he'd ever had, but the man had no sense of style, no appreciation for old-world elegance. He actually had a beanbag chair and a water bed in his apartment!

They were the odd couple of the department. Dark-man Dan, the conservative who regenerated best in complete aloneness. Rex, a lightweight from his blond hair to his sunny outlook. The predator and the people pleaser. In perfect balance right down to their egos. Whoever had the skill for a certain task took the initiative and dug in. Because of this solid foundation, Dan struggled for patience.

"Rex, I know you're trying to help. But please back off."

A blinking porch light caught his eye over Rex's shoulder. It was Timmy's last call. The child scooted up the front stoop with flailing arms.

Dan gripped the door handle of freedom. "Well, good night, Rex."

Rex chuckled knowingly. "Timmy was the last one, wasn't he?"

Dan's neck corded. "What?"

"The last one inside. I thought you were avoiding eye contact with me at first, but you've been keeping all six of them in range at the same time."

"Good night, Rex."

"I think I'll come in with you and call the auto-repair shop," Rex abruptly decided, shutting down the engine. "If my Fiero is ready, one of my neighbors can buzz me over there. Neighbors can be real assets sometimes."

Once they passed through the creaky front gate, it was obvious that someone had been up the walk before them.

"Expecting any visitors today, Danny?"

"No." Dan's dark blue eyes scanned the yard with a predator's keenness. The tracks were small. Made in the old crusted snow. They were filling now with the new flakes and were almost undetectable.

Working side by side for four years, the men had developed a telepathic connection. One glance settled things. It didn't appear serious, but they would take no chances. Dan led the way up the snow-powdered walk with a sure step, his system on alert. He seldom drew his gun, but it was resting snugly in his shoulder holster just in case.... He felt a huge responsibility to his neighbors—as many a policeman did. Despite his failings in the public-relations department, Dan was known as the neighborhood security blanket, the one to call at the first sign of peril. Or so the grapevine said, according to, and because of, the good Mrs. Nettel.

Cold air filled Dan's nostrils as he stomped up his stoop, mumbling under his breath. "Let it be a kid. Don't let it be a kid."

"You having a personal séance, or what?" Rex whispered in his ear.

Dan turned, his angled features fierce. "Just this once, I hope a little pest did have the nerve to crack the fence. I just hate to think he had the guts to break inside...."

Dan checked the door. By the shuffled mounds of
snow, it appeared that someone had tried to gain ac-
cess. Without success. Dan signaled to Rex and they
separated to circle either side of the house. Dan found
that every window in his path had been touched, small
fingertips pressed into the snowy sills, the ground
trampled by one presumably too short to comfortably
peer inside.

Rex was waiting for him at the back entrance, an odd
expression on his face. "You're gonna hate this."

Dan climbed the concrete steps, edging past Rex for
a look through the door pane trimmed with Mrs. Nettel's hand-sewn chiffon curtains. A half-empty milk jug
sat open on the table along with a cloudy glass. His
large blue ceramic crock was tipped on its side. Cookie
crumbs dashed with red and green sugar covered his
white tablecloth from end to end. Somebody had
feasted on his sister Gwen's precious spritzes.

"The Picasso of butter dough is not going to take this
news well," Rex predicted direly.

Dan jiggled the doorknob. Amazingly, it was still
locked.

"How on earth—"

Dan knew there was only one answer left. He
stomped to the cellar door closed flat against the
ground. "I've been meaning to seal this off permanently." The two wooden panels seemed to be secured
in the center by a padlock, but Dan demonstrated how
easily one panel lifted up from the hinge side. "As you
can see, it would take a mighty small intruder to slip
through here. Had to be a kid. A brave one," he added,
peering into the black bowels of his own basement.

"What do you say we use your key, partner," Rex proposed.

The pair found small tracks of melted snow all over the brown linoleum floor; originating from the gaping cellar door.

Dan shook his head. "I never leave this door ajar. It's freezing down there all year round. And I never leave these doors open, either," he raved in disgust, closing the yawning refrigerator and cupboards.

Someone had made a thorough search of the room. All of the crystal, china and antique bric-a-brac appeared undisturbed, however—more proof that they were dealing with a juvenile prankster. Some of the pieces Dan used every day were quite valuable. Even a rookie thief would suspect as much.

"Completely empty, Danny," Rex reported, tipping the blue jar upside down.

"There were ten dozen cookies in there!"

Rex righted the jar on the table with a thud. "Probably a kid in here on a dare. Just the same, we'll give this barn a once-over." As familiar with the house as if it were his own, Rex reached into the utility closet for Dan's giant flashlight and headed down to the cellar.

Dan, in turn, swiftly peeled off his bulky coat and headed for the mahogany staircase in the foyer. He ascended the creaky stairs gingerly, with only his penlight to guide him. Sensor-controlled night-lights along the upper hallway gave off just enough glow to show off the polish of the hardwood floor. There were six bedrooms in all, and two full baths. Dan entered them one by one, waving his thin beam into the air. Mrs. Nettel had been in for her biweekly cleaning. His late mother's sewing room was full of his freshly laundered and pressed clothing. The master suite next door smelled vaguely of lemon furniture polish, and the bed he'd stripped himself at dawn was now made, its fresh brown-and-tan covers taut.

Everything was spotless. Everything was undisturbed.

Except his private bathroom.

One flick of the penlight showed him the shambles! Dan groped for the light switch, then stood gaping at the moisture-sheened room, the soggy shower curtain, the slick floor, the soaked king-size towels. He advanced to pick up his best hairbrush, mysteriously entangled with very long, very blond strands of hair. He capped the open toothpaste tube oozing red gel on the vanity top.

If that wasn't enough! He looked down to find his own personal toothbrush floating in a puddle of water, frothed with use. That crossed the line somehow in Dan's mind, making this invasion unbearably intimate. And baffling. No child on a mad sugar-cookie spree would stop to clean up!

As Dan surveyed the room again, a mound of clothing lodged behind the door caught his eye. He scooped them up to find the oddest outfit imaginable for a Midwest winter's day. His bold visitor had arrived in a cellophane drugstore raincoat, a white denim sunsuit cut high on the hip. Nylon panties cut even higher on the hip. T-shirt and anklets in the same shade of mint green. And lastly, a pair of cookie-crumb-covered sneakers that might have been white at the time of purchase. He scanned the floor once again. No bra in sight.

His steel-trap mind devised a composite sketch of his intruder: a pint-size blond sugar junkie, breasts free of restraint.

Discomfort and Joy!

But where could she be? The house was silent, his bed empty.

Dan raced back to his bedroom for a closer look. This time his penlight spotted her, cuddled up in the window seat facing Pendham Avenue, sound asleep with a black fanny pack captured in her arms like a prized teddy bear.

Sweet, delectable Joy. So beautiful in slumber. So beguiling in nothing but his white terry-cloth robe.

Elation and frustration nearly choked him as he moved to the bedside table to turn on a lamp. How dare she make herself at home after what she'd pulled last Christmas? His internal defenses signaled him to back off, to take time out to cope.

Then a low seductive moan sliced the silence as she twisted in the cramped confines of her nest, luring him back to the window seat.

It was a trap. And he'd walked right into it!

'It was one of her games of seduction. She'd deliberately set the scene for their reunion in his bedroom.

Ready to break her fall, he watched as she sought comfort in the cramped cushioned cocoon, burrowing and curling like a kitten with scrubbed pink skin and fluffy reams of fragrant blond hair. The sash tied at her waist slackened with her every move until the robe gaped open below the waist to reveal a glimpse of luscious thigh and a nest of true blond curls.

It was enough to make a grown man weep with desire. Joy was a masterpiece of nature. One he'd thoroughly adored, inch by inch. She was tiny in every way a woman could be. Oh, how big she'd made him feel....

Dan felt a betraying ache below the belt. How he wanted nothing more than to feel big inside her all over again.

Joy belonged in bed and fully expected him to put her there. He scooped her up in his arms, marveling, not for the first time, at how light she was despite her incessant appetite. Her hair poured over his arm like liquid gold and her tiny mouth curved in a secret smile. A head full of dreams and schemes. What did she want with him this time? What was she going to do to him this time? He stood there cradling her, feeling a slight familiar rumble beneath his feet, as though he was standing on the seat of a roller coaster. He closed his eyes. It was all coming back now, the soaring senses, the thudding in heart and ears. The climb. Up, up the narrow track, far beyond reason.

No safety bar. No brakes. No speed limit.

Not on this ride. The Joyride.

Dan's eyes snapped open as Joy released a sleepy murmur. Where was his head? Rex was still downstairs. If he caught him in a clinch like this, Dan would never hear the end of it. He stumbled toward the bed.

Tuck her in. There would be plenty of time to play this out later on....

He froze again. Was that red sugar on her breast?

Dan peeled back the robe's lapel for a peek. Sure enough, traces of crumbled cookie clung to her shower-moist skin—to the very tip of her rosy nipple. But how? She'd feasted down at the kitchen table, then presumably showered.... And she knew he'd wonder. A bit of mystery in the game. Dan dipped his mouth to the soft mound of flesh and grazed his tongue in the banquet of crumbs. She was delicious. He gently suckled her sweetened nipple, then withdrew with a start.

How easily he was ambushed! How much he had missed her!

With a surge of resistance, Dan again moved for the mattress. To his surprise, the sash gave out completely. The robe fell open, as if weighted with lead.

But it wasn't lead. It was cookies. About three dozen of them. He understood now. Joy had munched herself to sleep. Rather than leave some of those painstakingly crafted spritzes down in the jar, Joy had smuggled them upstairs. Crumbs were everywhere, he realized. And Joy knew that Dan never allowed food out of the kitchen, not even in the safe house!

She had thoughtlessly helped herself. As usual, acting on passion rather than common sense. A clear reminder of why things would never work between them; why their relationship could never progress beyond the senses. How could he so desperately desire such a careless woman?

Well, his sheets would not be just another tablecloth, he decided with resolve, peeling the robe off her with a magician's flourish. He tossed it in the hamper and her on the mattress with an unceremonious plop.

Through it all, she slept on with a faraway mumble. Tucking her naked form beneath the snugly pulled covers, he fumed that this certainly was not the scenario he'd envisioned over and over again while on dreary stakeout duty—the cool, collected cop facing the hot, contrite babe who only wanted forgiveness.

She'd bested him in the bedroom all over again—without even bothering to wake up.

3

All snug in his bed

DAN HIT THE STAIRS AT a gallop, pausing in the drafty foyer below to collect his senses. What an effort it was! He'd pulled off life-threatening sting operations with far more finesse.

Conversational murmurings emanated from the study on the left. Rex was most likely on the phone with his mechanic. Though Dan had long ago accepted Rex's interference in his life as part of the territory, his obsession with Joy was so private, so personal, so difficult to rationalize to himself, he wanted to work it out with her alone.

With his shoulders squared, Dan rounded the doorway. His flamboyant partner was seated at the rolltop desk, his ear clamped to the telephone receiver, his scuffed shoes propped up on the fine wood surface of the antique.

Rex cupped the mouthpiece at the sight of him. "Everything okay?"

"All secure," Dan replied smoothly. He waited until Rex hung up seconds later. "Your Fiero ready?"

"Yeah," he affirmed, not moving a muscle. "You know, Danny, you really should nail that cellar shut permanently."

Dan strode forward, lifting Rex's feet off the gleaming desktop, buffing the surface with his hankie. "I will. First thing tomorrow."

Rex righted himself in the creaky chair. "That doesn't sound like my overachiever buddy."

Dan met his doubtful look blankly. A few questions and a couple of deductions and the snoop would have this sorted out.

"It'll be an easier job to tackle in the daylight," he claimed, strolling over to unobtrusively draw the drapes over the windows facing the street and Mrs. Nettel's house to the north. He fought the desire to tear from room to room, sealing up every pane.

Hidden treasure. Joy was his own hidden treasure.

"Will you be picking up your car tonight?"

"Plenty of time. Open till ten." Rex stood, stretching with a huge yawn.

"Well, thanks for backing me up in here. One never knows—"

"Hey, what are partners for? You'd have covered me in the same circumstances."

Dan frowned as Rex wandered over to the mantel and began to thumb through the Christmas cards that Mrs. Nettel had so neatly arranged. "What are you doing?"

"Going through these again. I can't believe all the high-level politicians who think to send greetings to little ole you."

"Connections from my father's years in the Senate."

"I suppose all of the same old bigwigs will be here Sunday for your shindig." When Dan nodded he added, "Too bad you don't jazz it up a little. Invite some of the guys from our softball team."

"The reception is a tradition started by my parents," Dan needlessly reminded. "A certain dignity is expected. Gwen and I have seen to it for years."

"Hey, just a bleepin' minute," Rex demanded. "Where's Joy's card? Stashed between your pillows for sweet dreams, or what?"

If only he knew what was stashed up in his bed! "It's gotta be there someplace, Rex," he cajoled mildly.

"I tell ya, boy, it's vanished!"

Dan shrugged. "I didn't move it. Maybe it slipped behind a chair."

"In this sterile joint?" Rex moved back to the desk and grabbed the stack of empty envelopes that Dan kept for their return addresses. Each year Dan faithfully double-checked each sender's residence against his Christmas list. "Envelope's gone, too. What do you think it means?"

Dan met Rex's interrogative look with a flicker of annoyance. "Maybe it means that someone close to me would rather I forget about Joy."

"Not me!" Rex denied. "I said you should go after her, remember?" Dan clenched his hands at his sides in an effort to control his temper. Would this guy ever go home? "You and Gwen put me through the ringer about Joy on Saturday and enough's enough!"

"But it does seem strange—"

"My money's on Gwen," Dan cut in. "She's been trying to run my life since my Pablum days. Or maybe Mrs. Nettel mislaid it while dusting. I really don't give a damn either way."

"Hey, I'm sorry," Rex said. "I was only trying to defend your right to a wild and woolly affair to Gwen. The chemistry between you and Joy is sort of intriguing. Guess we did go overboard with our debate. As for the card, my instincts must be working overtime."

"Well, it's hard to shut the system down at night sometimes," Dan relented on a calmer note.

"You're gonna laugh at me, Danny," Rex cautioned. "But for a second or two there, I thought maybe Joy was back."

The bastard of a best friend was unbelievably shrewd. "Why, Rex?"

"I don't know." Rex shrugged, attempting to rearrange the cards on the mantel. "The footprints, the cookies."

"Oh." He feigned sudden enlightenment. "See what you mean."

Rex stepped back to look at his awkward handiwork, beaming over the hodgepodge. "Just a hunch that didn't pan out. A shame, too, considering how she lit your fire."

"I know exactly where she is now—thanks to the card," Dan was quick to clarify. "And will handle her as I see fit." As a matter of fact, he was on the verge of having a fit over handling her!

"Okay, okay," Rex conceded. "But you and I both know she's out of danger and could be picked up in Orlando within a few hours' time."

Dan folded his arms across his chest. "Uh-huh."

"And she sent the card to see if it's okay to come back."

Dan saluted him. "Thank you, Dear Abby."

Rex studied him for a moment. "Hey, what's on your chin?"

"Where? What?" Dan's fingers connected with some sugar crystals lodged in his five o'clock shadow.

"I didn't think there was a spritz left in the house."

Caught with the evidence! "Even the crumbs aren't bad. Plenty of those left."

"Guess so. If you're that hungry, Danny, maybe we should raid your icebox, have a snifter of your treasured brandy." Rex rubbed his hands together in anticipation. "What do you say?"

The telephone rang as Dan sought for an excuse. Maybe this was the out he needed. It wasn't. An unrecognizable voice asked if it was the Pizza Pantry.

"No, it isn't," Dan replied. He was about to disconnect when a bolt of inspiration struck him. If he played it right he could get rid of Rex the easy way, after all— under his own steam! "No, it isn't," he repeated, "*Mrs. Nettel.* Your sixth sense was correct." He held the phone close as Rex watched him with interest. "The footprints may have seemed innocent, but I'm afraid we had a small break-in over here today. Don't be upset, dear. You can't watch every minute. No, the mess isn't too bad. Just cookie crumbs and some melted snow.... Pop next door now?"

Rex's mouth dropped. Dan shrugged at him helplessly. "Tomorrow is soon enough...." Rex nodded, moving for the leather easy chair in the corner. "But if you insist ..." Dan bit his lip to force down a laugh as Rex's butt froze in midair over the chair. The clown deserved to be jerked around for snooping into his affairs.

"Is she or isn't she?" Rex demanded as Dan replaced the receiver.

"One never knows with her," Dan pondered, staring off into space.

"She'll be over," Rex decided, hastily easing his brown topcoat back over his suit. "Sorry I can't stay. Watching that old fussbudget fuss over you is too much. And when she's done with you, she starts picking the lint off *my* clothes. You know how I hate for anybody but you to do that!"

Dan opened the door as Rex charged across the foyer. "Thanks again, buddy."

"I'll swing by for you 'round seven," Rex promised. He paused on the stoop, wagging a finger. "Be sure you get to bed early tonight. You really need some shut-eye."

"I'm headed straight for the bedroom," Dan proclaimed, shutting the door on his openmouthed partner. After a brief pause, he realized that was the wrong thing to say, with Mrs. Nettel supposedly stopping by and all. But so what? Rex was on the right side of the door—the outside! And Joy was on the inside, all safe and sound after a year out in the cold.

There was a lightness in his step as Dan took the stairs this time. A merry merry Christmas was possible after all.

JOY AWOKE TO THE SIGHT of Dan, seated in a large wing chair by the fireplace, rummaging through her waist sack. She rubbed her eyes with her fists, wondering for a moment if she was dreaming of him again. But the roaring fire at his side licked and crackled with a burst of heat that reached the bed, convincing her that it was indeed real.

His angular profile looked pretty darn wonderful in the shadows, she decided after a long hard look. For the first time in ages she felt completely safe—not an easy

admission for a independent woman to make. But
Dan's presence always dominated a room. His mas-
culinity enhanced her femininity in a powerful, fasci-
nating way. She shivered slightly despite the heat.

"Hey, that's private property, copper," she huskily
chided in greeting.

Dan rose from the chair and wandered over to the
bed with the sack in hand. "Anybody who uses my
toothbrush, and lets me caress her—"

"Okay, okay," she blurted out with a wave. "Dig in
my purse."

"Not much in it, anyway," he said, tossing it on the
bedside table. He wandered around the bed, his solid
shoulders stiff beneath his white dress shirt. To Dan,
relaxing was loosening his tie and undoing his collar
button. Joy was glad he'd removed his ever-present
shoulder holster. He wasn't going to like what she had
to tell him. The fewer weapons at his disposal, the better!

"Guess I'm out of everything these days," she admitted. "Luck. Time. Money."

"Clothes too, it seems," Dan added, gesturing to the
heap on the chair.

"I can explain everything," she assured him defensively. And she would have, if she hadn't suddenly
tented the covers with her knees and realized she was
naked. Her wide accusatory eyes met Dan's gleaming
blue ones.

"I had to confiscate the robe as evidence."

Joy's gaze fell as the sheet slipped down her breasts
an inch. "Looks like you cleaned up everything."

"Best trap you ever laid."

Joy traced her lips with her tongue. "Give me back the cookies and we'll do it all over again."

"They were full of fuzz so I threw them away."

"You didn't!" she exclaimed.

"Forget it, Joy," Dan cautioned, his patience slipping. "You've had enough! Taken enough!"

Joy gulped. Did he mean she'd taken too much for granted? Dan left nothing to chance; had continually criticized her impetuous moves, as well. Maybe returning to him this way was the biggest blooper of them all. But the idea of Dan not wanting her, of finding her undesirable, was totally devastating. If she'd learned one thing while out on her own, it was that he gave her an appealing sense of stability. Yes, he was conservative, pigheaded, and often downright too introverted to reach, but he suited her.

In a shaky voice she asked him for the truth. "Danny, are you mad that I came back?"

"I'm mad because you left in the first place," he said. "There is a difference, Joy. Do you understand the difference?"

"Of course I do! I'm sorry I had to go," she hurriedly explained. "But you were going to wreck my whole life."

"I was going to protect you in the best way I knew how."

The fact that her flight shattered him personally and professionally was something he wasn't proud of. To this day, he didn't understand how she'd managed to slip beyond his control. She was like a low-grade fever, a mild lingering burn—almost undetectable much of the time.

And now it looked like he was in for one hell of a flare-up. To his credit, he was smart enough to acknowledge her seductive powers. The mere sight of her tonight had him hot and bothered, and just plain bothered. How could she tempt and annoy him at the same time—with the same weapons? It seemed he couldn't live with her or without her.

Fueled by anger, he aimed an accusatory finger at her. "You should've taken the last step under my guidance. Gone in the Witness Protection Program. That way—" He broke off, swallowing. "That way, I would've known where you were, and could've checked up on you."

"I'm so sorry if I caused you worry," she said softly.

"Worry?" His black brows drew in a hard line over his nose. "You ripped my heart out and took it with you."

"I did?" She smiled through misty eyes.

"You don't need to look so smug about it," he griped, sitting on the mattress beside her.

"I'm just so happy to be here," she blurted out honestly.

"You're lucky to be here, you mean. Why, you didn't even dye your hair," he scolded, raking his fingers through the rippling tide on her shoulder.

Joy shivered as his roughened palm grazed the tender side of her breast. The sheet was rumpled in her lap now. "I couldn't bear to color it," she confided. "Do you know how few real blondes there are left on this planet?"

"No," he retorted. "And I don't know how many are left on *your* planet, either."

Joy wrinkled her nose. "Hey, it just so happens that I was clever enough to find a wig that gives me a whole new look. See what it's done for Shakespeare," she invited with a gesture. "Crazy, huh?"

Dan tore his eyes from her bust to the marble one of the playwright, which sat on a pedestal beside his dresser. Its profile had lost much of its nobility with the tousled mop of red hair atop its head. "Point taken," he relented. "Thank goodness you won't be needing it anymore."

Oh, wouldn't she? But that was a truth to face tomorrow, in the stark daylight. As exigent as the danger was, there was a more pressing need blooming within her—the need for physical contact. Dan was aching for her too, she knew. The fingers grazing her hair and face were shaking with electricity.

"Touch me, Danny," she invited in a heavy, sweet voice.

A heartbeat later she was in his arms. Then, back into the pillows, the smoothness of his shirt grazing her nipples as they sank down. The weight of his large frame on her small form was a comforting crush; his mouth locking on hers was sweeter than any sugar treat could be.

Joy couldn't move an inch, pinned beneath his length. She wanted to wiggle free in a burst of energy, wind her legs around his hips, cajole every stitch of clothing off him. But she knew Dan to be a meticulous man in every way. A leisurely seducer who believed in long, tempting foreplay. Thorough to a fault.

"It's all over, you know," he rasped in her ear. "You took a helluva chance coming back unannounced, but it's all right."

Leave it to him to go on thinking! He was spoiling it all. Raising herself on her elbows, she took the bait. "Okay, copper, what do you mean?"

Dan tore his mouth from her throat, hovering over her with a surprised look. "I mean that the last two villains were caught. Turns out they were cops, just like my informant Repeat said."

With impressive strength she pushed him off her. He landed beside her on the mattress with a thump. "Hey, I thought you'd be easy tonight of all nights," he complained in bewilderment.

"When did this happen, Danny?"

Dan shrugged. "About six months ago. If you'd been in the federal program, we could've yanked you out way back then."

So who was after her in Orlando? A shiver coursed her spine. Joy tugged at the covers for warmth.

Dan stroked the hollow of her cheek. "What's the matter, honey?"

"Oh, Dan, I hoped we could make mindless love, like we used to."

Dan nibbled at her ear. "It's just pillow talk. Nothing that can't wait." He shifted his leg over hers, inching apart her thighs with his knee.

Oh, how she longed for his caress. His hair-roughened skin invading the silky bow of her legs was enough to send her into outer space! But she knew she'd burst if she didn't tell him of her predicament. "There's still someone after me, Danny!"

Their eyes met in a single flash of shock and panic. Any hope Joy had of a simple, reasonable explanation was snuffed then and there. He didn't know a thing about it. When she hung her head, Dan seized her by the shoulders and gave her a gentle shake. "Tell me everything."

The sensuality soon dissipated from his handsome face, leaving Dan nothing but a demanding cop. Joy struggled to mask her disappointment.

"Well, I sent you the card last week. Then I waited." She fingered the edge of the sheet. "I sorta hoped you'd come for me."

"And, and," he prodded.

"Would you ever have come for me?" she persisted bleakly.

"I barely had a chance! Now tell me, what happened next?"

"Somebody showed up at my apartment house, claiming to be my cousin—Faye Fairway's cousin, I mean. Talked to my landlord, Henry Sheldon."

"What did he look like?"

"The person was in a disguise. Good enough to distort gender."

Dan threw up his hands. "I don't believe this!"

"It's all true. And it's all your fault!" Joy burst into tears, and covered her face with her hands.

Dan stared at her, incredulous. "*My* fault?"

"Yes," she sobbed through muffling palms. "Whoever it was got all the information he needed from the Christmas card I sent you. Faye was a brand-new character I'd created for my act before the trial. Nobody knew about her yet."

The misplaced card Rex couldn't find. That had been the link? It was difficult to believe that Joy's whereabouts were tracked down through something in his own home!

Joy easily read the brooding doubt on his face. "All the facts came from that card, Danny. The way my feet have been sore, my homesickness, everything."

"Wonder if you were followed here . . ." he pondered grimly.

"I doubt it, with the zigzag route I took."

"Think this person broke into your place, Joy? Maybe he was after something."

"I thought of that, too," Joy confessed. "So when I called Mr. Sheldon to tell him I was safe with a friend, I asked him."

"Did you give away your location?" he cut in sharply.

"No, of course not!" Joy huffed. "And he still thinks I'm Faye Fairway. Anyway, he said the person never came back after I fled. And that he'll be keeping a sharp eye on my apartment, as well. But face it, Danny, I don't have anything of value. Just a waist sack full of personal stuff, an old car, and my trunk of belongings in your storage garage. It's me this stalker wants!"

Dan reluctantly recognized that his home was the last place Joy should be. "Sending the card was a great idea," he began slowly. "It . . . eased my mind concerning you more than I can say." Her face brightened slightly, making it heart-wrenching to continue. "But to make a beeline back here to the source of the trouble, to deliberately return to the danger zone . . . It was so careless, so unbelievably impulsive. You should've called ahead for direction."

"I feel, I act," Joy cried in defense. "It's the way I keep life simple."

"Living on hundred-proof emotion makes life far more complicated!" Dan objected. And not for the first time. On every occasion that they'd interacted on anything higher than basic instinct, the differences in their personalities had rapidly surfaced.

"You don't want to help me anymore," she said. "Now that I've done my duty in court, you don't want to protect me! Someone may be out to kill me!"

Dan forced his temper down his throat. He was once again storming down the ribbon of road that had so divided them, that had originally driven her away. He couldn't protect her properly if he couldn't keep her close. "We don't know for sure that someone is trying to kill you," he attempted to console on a gentler note. "Jerome Berkley is out of the way, serving a fifty-year sentence in Illinois."

Joy regarded him with a horrified look. "He killed his own wife because she knew about his illegal activities!"

"Yes, but he was trying to protect his dirty operation at the Laff Trak," Dan explained. "It's all over for him. Harming you wouldn't get him anywhere. Sources tell me he's a model prisoner, that he's hoping for eventual parole."

"Oh? Well, I'll bet Theo Nelson's still furious with me for squealing on him," she fretted, crushing in her fingers the tie hanging loosely around Dan's neck.

Dan tenderly cupped her face. "If somebody had wanted you dead in Orlando, you'd be dead." It was stark comfort, but a fact.

"Then it's crazy, Dan!"

"Seems so on the surface," he conceded. "But there is an answer. There always is. Finding it is the only way either of us is ever going to live in peace."

Joy puckered her lips mournfully. "You don't want to do it anymore, do you?"

As distracting as Joy was, Dan's focus had shifted to the dangers surrounding her. Succumbing to Joy's charms when he'd been supposed to be protecting her had grown into a symbol of utter carelessness in his mind. A failure to perform his duty. "Calling sex 'it' is doing yourself a grave injustice, honey," he eventually said thickly, sliding his hands down her silky shoulders.

"I know what you're thinking, Danny," she whispered. "Everything would be different if you hadn't crossed the line on duty, hadn't started making love to me in the first place."

Dan had forgotten how insightful she could be. "I will always wonder about it, I guess. Would I have been sharper all along? Would we have caught those two last stragglers in Berkley's criminal network before the trial?" Dan exhaled heavily over the weighted question. "You wouldn't have had to go away at all, then."

"It's all fate, Danny. There's no sense in your beating every wrong move with a club."

Dan's expression grew inscrutable, but he was nonplussed by her scolding remark. Is that how she viewed him? As a dark, moody cop obsessed with his every move? Could he make love to a woman who had such an opinion of him? He wasn't sure her opinion should matter, especially if "fate" had nothing special in store for the pair of them. The only thing he was certain of, was that he wasn't going to reach any rational conclusions tonight.

"What you really need more than anything else right now is my full and undivided platonic attention," he said quietly.

"What I really need right now is a hug," she admitted tentatively. "Would . . . Would you hold me without the rest, Danny?"

The truth about their past relationship hit him between the eyes with that one. He'd never held her without intercourse before. The very idea caused a tremor to course his body. He suddenly felt like a teenage boy attempting his first move.

Joy's face grew distraught over his brief hesitation. "If you don't—"

"Of course I do." He busied himself for a moment, fluffing the pillows against the walnut headboard. She meekly crawled into his lap and snuggled up against his chest. Dan couldn't believe the many facets she'd already revealed during her short visit. Playful seductress, bold temptress, angry accuser, and now, finally, scared woman.

"I'm so frightened," she offered in excuse. "But I know I'm safe with you. Does that make any sense?"

"Yeah, it does." He rubbed the length of her creamy back in a gentle massaging motion, relaxing himself as she loosened in his arms. Joy was really back. In his hands. Despite all the trauma, an odd inner peace settled in the pit of his stomach.

"Go to sleep, honey," he murmured into her hair.

"I will. Tell me again about your lovely Christmas traditions, so I can dream about them."

Dan rolled his eyes above her with a sigh. "Well . . ."

"How about your tree? I never did take the time to look for it downstairs."

Dan drew a hesitant breath. "It, ah, isn't set up yet."

Joy opened one eye and regarded him suspiciously. "Who does it? Gwen?"

"Decorators. From a department store downtown."

"Yuck."

"Works for me. Makes things predictable and simple."

Joy grinned sleepily. "That must mean I haven't missed your annual Christmas party yet."

"It's Sunday."

"Then I got here just in time...."

Dan watched Joy fall asleep, knowing she'd be dreaming of the Christmas that never really was at the Burke Castle.

4

Foes you know and mistletoe

JOY WANDERED INTO THE kitchen Thursday morning just as Dan was barreling through the back door in the wake of a cold gust. He was already dressed for work in a gray suit and his uniform white shirt.

"Kind of brisk out there," he greeted, pushing the door shut with his shoulder.

Joy inhaled with a squeak as chilly air shot up beneath the baggy sweatshirt serving as her pajamas. "Slept in the buff in Florida."

"I imagine it was a lot more comfortable there," he acquiesced, dragging his feet across the small entry rug with more care than seemed necessary.

Joy's teeth sank into her lower lip as she surveyed his mood. She wasn't registering a complaint of any kind. She was exactly where she wanted to be. Dan was the most capable bodyguard imaginable. And the most intriguing man she'd ever known.

Though she'd tried all year long, she'd been unable to shake him from her mind. There were so many loose ends left hanging when she took flight after the trial. Being apart from Dan all those months had only enhanced her curiosity over what might have been.

Forever the optimist, Joy was determined to look on the bright side. Yes, her life was in danger again, but

Dan would soon square that. And she was in for the
Christmas of her dreams—the one he'd promised her
last year—right in his beautiful home. What better setting to explore her true feelings for this hunky, com-
plex cop?

But did he want these same things? She wasn't even
sure she was welcome. Admittedly, this was the
strangest "morning after" she'd ever experienced. She
shifted uneasily on her bare feet as he pulled the shade
on the back-door window. What should she say? *You
were great last night, baby. It was the first time in my
entire life that someone held me without amorous intent.* As much as she'd wanted him to seduce her, she'd
appreciated his gesture of compassion. She'd been so
tired, so vulnerable, so unsure about what she wanted.
Now, in the light of day, she had a more solid perspec-
tive on their predicament. Or *her* predicament—de-
pending upon his outlook.

"They confiscate your gun, copper?" she teased with
a forced lilt, gesturing to the hammer still clutched in
his hand.

"No, just nailing up the cellar once and for all," he
explained, hanging the tool back on its designated peg
in the utility closet. "Put slide bolts on the inside of the
front and back doors, too. That should help keep a
tighter rein on any visitors who may show up."

Visitors? He may just as well have said "intruders,"
by the tone of his voice. And she'd done more than
"show up," hadn't she? She'd gone the whole nine
yards, right down to robe and toothbrush. Maybe he
was just out of patience with her. "I've been thinking
about last night," she ventured as he eased by on his
way to the refrigerator.

"Oh?" His back was to her as he rooted around the items on the top shelf. It seemed aeons before he took out a jug of milk.

To her indignation, he walked by her without comment, and seated himself at the table.

"Maybe I should just go!" she said, causing him to snap her a startled glance.

"That's ridiculous, Joy!"

"Isn't that what you're thinking?"

"No, no," he denied, raking loose strands of raven hair that had fallen across his brow.

"Last night you said my coming here was a wrong move," she challenged.

"That was the objective cop in me talking."

"So who was holding me all night long, Danny? The cop? The lover? Who was that man?"

Dan shook his head in bewilderment. He didn't know himself! And he was a man who thought he knew his own mind. To think he ever believed himself to be totally over Joy was laughable. Those same old feelings had surged through his system at the mere sight of her, and they seemed to have intensified with age, like a fine wine. But how could he explain his befuddlement? The last thing he wanted to do was insult her with a half-hearted attempt.

Fury mounted in Joy. "I don't know why I ever thought I'd be welcome here in the first place," she finally blurted out. "I'm going upstairs to get my stuff. In the meantime, you can decide which door I should use!"

Dan's hand shot out and snagged her wrist.

"Let go of me!" She hurled herself backward to escape his grip.

Dan sprang to his feet, knocking his chair over in an effort to detain her. "You're staying right here until we clear up this mess!" He stilled her batting arms by pinning her against his length.

"You sure have fast reflexes for a deep thinker, copper!"

Dan was panting slightly from the tussle, his tie and jacket a little askew. "In your case, guess I've always grabbed first and thought later."

Joy had given up the struggle completely. Tilting her misty green eyes up to his blazing blue ones she asked the frightening question that had lingered in her mind the whole night through. "How can you help me if you don't even know how you feel about me?"

"I've guarded many a body without pausing to examine my feelings," he growled back, his fingers digging into her shoulders. "Believe me, it's the easy route."

"It's way too late for us to take the easy way out. After the closeness we shared . . ."

Dan closed his eyes for a moment of calm. She was right. It never went down easy with them. Never would.

"Okay, okay," he began between breaths as she tried to shake free. "I'll tell you what I am sure of. You were right to put your trust in me again. We have a lot of unfinished business—"

"And it isn't all official," she broke in as if to check.

"No, no, it isn't," he admitted. "Joy, what I'm trying to say is that I wouldn't trust anyone else to watch over you. So, make yourself at home."

"Oh, thank heavens, Danny," she enthused with a sniff. "To be honest, there is no one else—noplace else for me."

"How about scrambling us up a cup of coffee," he said gently, tipping his head toward the steaming carafe on the counter.

She gave his lapel a pat. "Right away, copper. It just so happens I've poured many a cup as Faye Fairway this year. You just sit down at the table."

"Thanks." He righted his chair with a steadying sigh and sank down at the round oak table.

The cellar and bolts hadn't been his only sunrise chores. The white tablecloth was free of cookie crumbs and the table was set for two, with bowls, spoons and napkins. A variety of cereals, milled from only the healthiest grains, was lined up in a wall of boxes.

Knowing that Dan was watching her every move, Joy lazily swayed toward the counter. With her hopes refreshed, she focused her sights on her goals once more. It was only right that they rekindle their affair. She didn't believe for a minute that their intimacy had hampered his performance. If anything, their lovemaking had only heightened Dan's senses. Made him cop dynamite. The way the rest of it played out was fate, pure and simple. He had to learn to take his pleasures with less forethought.

"Here we are," she announced as she lifted two steaming mugs up and over the cereal boxes with practiced motion.

"You're an angel," he murmured distractedly as he took a mug in his hands.

Angel? Joy wrinkled her nose. Not the naughty image she was looking for at the moment. Pressing her thighs together, she slid into the chair at his right. "I don't have any panties on, copper," she purred, leaning close with her chin propped in her hand.

"A deduction I've already reached," he admitted evenly, filling his bowl with flakes, dousing them with milk. "But something we can surely fix."

A burning coil of desire flared, causing her to fidget on her smooth wooden seat. "Yeah?"

"But you need nourishment first." Dan shoveled cereal into his mouth and waved his spoon at her. "Eat."

Joy glanced at the boxes with disinterest, reluctantly choosing some wheat minibiscuits with a pitiful film of frosting on them. She poured a few into her bowl. Dan tilted the box, forcing out several more.

"Where's the sugar bowl?" she asked.

"Don't have one," Dan claimed.

Joy frowned. "The hell you don't! I saw it myself yesterday. It's real pretty, too. Rose-colored glass. Filled to the brim."

"Joy, sugar makes you all the more hyper. It's not a good idea to pile it on everything."

Joy cast a feeble look down at her steaming mug. "Not even a sprinkle for my coffee?"

Dan added a dollop of milk to her brew. "It's very good this way."

Joy took a sip, frowning over the bitter taste. "I suppose I'll be needing a house key," she mused, "now that you've buttoned up this place tighter than a drum."

Dan's black brows arched over the barricade of boxes. "I installed the slide bolts to keep you safe while you are on the inside. A key won't open them."

"Still, if I am to stay... If you want me to feel at home..."

"At home on the *inside*, honey," he firmly insisted. "You are confined to the house, for now. We can't risk someone discovering your location."

"Guess you've got a point," she surrendered.

"A damn good point."

Joy slurped and stared, waiting for some conversation, some reaction. Nothing. His jaw was pulled taut with every chew, his eyes trained on an unknown spot in the floral wallpaper. He was hopelessly buried in one of his deep trances. "Danny, I'll go nuts if you don't start sharing your thoughts with me!"

Dan tasted his coffee with a grim nod. "I'm thinking about your Christmas card. I can't believe it's the link between you and the stalker. But the evidence is indisputable," he hastily admitted. "Add to it the fact that the card has disappeared from my mantel—"

"You had my card out in the open?" she gasped, lunging forth to grab his wrist as he dug back into his cereal.

"Well, Mrs. Nettel took it off my desk and arranged it with the others," he explained. "But it seemed harmless enough at the time, considering that I thought this Berkley ordeal was over."

"How many possible suspects do we have here? Twenty? A hundred?"

"Three."

"Oh." Joy sank back in her chair, releasing her grip. The poor lug. No wonder he was such a brooding mess this morning. "All your people, huh?"

"Yes," he begrudgingly admitted. "Rex and Gwen were here on Saturday to do the spritzes."

"And this Mrs. Nettel person is the third," Joy finished. "Exactly who is she?"

Dan smiled. "She is my next-door neighbor. Has been for nearly a year."

"Her age?" she drilled.

"Fifty-five if she's a day." Dan reached over to tweak her nose. "We have a comfortable, chatty relationship. She does the cleaning here on Wednesdays and Saturdays and is deeply interested in my police work."

Joy squinted warily. "A lot of middle-aged women are looking mighty good these days."

"She's no vamp trying to jump my bones, Joy," Dan assured with a chuckle. "She's best described as a motherly armchair detective and great neighbor."

Joy straightened her spine. "Oh, I'll bet she has one, though!"

"One what?" Dan balked.

"A key, a key, you louse!"

"Mrs. Nettel has no key," Dan hastily reassured. Only Joy Jones could go from doubting her welcome to wheedling for a house key in a matter of minutes!

"Well, at least let me be the vamp trying to jump your bones. I won't even rumple your suit," she guaranteed huskily, her complexion luminous with desire.

Dan's body pulsed as her fingernail scraped across the top of his stiff shirt-collar. She could make good the offer. Had done so every morning before court. It had been one of their last games at the hotel. Frisk the officer—without so much as a wrinkle.

"Now, Joy, this is a good example of what I cannot do right now. If I slip into game playing, I'll be totally lost in you."

The admission brought a feline smile to her lips. "Sounds wonderful. Just like old times in the safe house when—"

"In the safe house we were cut off from the world," he interjected firmly. "We aren't isolated this time. I have to go out into the world and function." When she pouted he added, "We were a great team there, for a while. You cooperated all the way and together we sent a killer to prison. I want you to follow my lead again. Let's settle this mess, once and for all."

"I did a whole lot of other things you asked me to, copper," she reminded in a silky whisper.

Dan knew that she was trying to recapture the magic between them and he was deeply touched by it. He reached up to squeeze the hand still skimming his neck. "I'm an equal-rights guy when it comes down to mattress matches, honey. But I'm a chauvinistic policeman when it concerns business. It's best to keep duty and desire separate for now. Trust me to know my limits. And be satisfied to know that you are the ultimate distraction to me."

"Ha! I'm beginning to think I just don't hold your interest as a lover anymore."

"Liar." He drew her hand to his mouth, kissing her palm, her pulse point, eventually placing it back on the table after an obvious internal struggle.

"I almost had ya there, copper," she teased beguilingly.

"You sure did," he admitted with a measure of surprise. "But don't go getting your panties in a twist about it."

"I have no panties to twist, remember? No tops, no bottoms, no deodorant, no toothbrush of my own. Solve that problem, Detective Burke!"

"Gwen still keeps some things in her old bedroom for convenience," Dan replied with a twinkle in his eye. "First door at the top of the stairs."

Joy leaped up in all her five feet. "She's almost as tall as you are!"

"Somewhere between you and me, I'd say," Dan argued sensibly.

"Her stuff will fall right off me."

Dan dabbed his mouth with his napkin, attempting to hide a wry grin. "Oh. Well, there are some boxes of clothing I've been collecting from churches and schools for shipment overseas up there, too. Must be stuff of all sizes in that lot. And there are enough toiletries around here to start a hotel," he stated with finality. "Leaving you no reason whatsoever to venture out, no use for a key."

Joy stood fuming over him, hands on hips. Dan's eyes dropped from her discontented face to her hip, where the sweatshirt was slowly edging up to reveal a glimpse of luscious rump.

"You know what I really need, don't you?"

Dan's expression tightened with resolve. "A sound spanking comes to mind."

"No! No! My trunk, fool, my trunk!" she proclaimed triumphantly. "All of my costumes from my act are in there, as well as stage makeup and many little personal belongings." She clamped on to his shoulders and gave him a shake. "Get my trunk out of storage and I'll be satisfied."

Dan made a dubious noise. "Now who's making promises she can't keep? Besides, that garage is way out of my way and my caseload is already overloaded."

"Well, you're going to make time to track down Repeat, aren't you?" she challenged. "See if he has anything new on the Berkley case?"

"You're getting pretty good at this detective stuff," he begrudged her.

Joy raised her tiny chin proudly. "I'll give armchair detective Mrs. Nettel a run for her money."

"I know," he conceded wearily.

"Well, when you ditch Rex to talk to Repeat, stop by the storage place for my trunk."

"I'll try, Joy."

"Thanks, Danny." Joy couldn't resist easing onto his lap, coiling her arms around his neck. Poor man. She'd never met a one so in need of closeness and affection. "I know this will be a tough day, keeping this secret from Rex and all."

"Knowing he may be keeping some secrets of his own makes it easier. You just concentrate on staying out of trouble," he directed, pushing strands of her silky hair from her face. With a grimace he added, "I just hope we can find a way to keep you here incognito. There's the party on Sunday. And Mrs. Nettel's twice-a-week cleanup."

Joy straightened her spine, prepared to make the ultimate sacrifice. "I'm staying put, even if I have to clean this place myself!"

"Well, it would be nice if you straightened up the bathroom. But to dismiss Mrs. N., to make any changes in my routine, would be a red flag to the enemy."

"You're right, of course." Joy bit her lip thoughtfully.

"We'll plan our strategy together when I return tonight," he vowed with a harried look at the clock. "Rex

will be here any minute, and I want to keep him outside. Now be sure to stay away from the doors and let
the machine pick up all my calls. If I want to talk to you
I'll leave a message that way." When Dan tried to shift
her off his thighs, she clung all the more.

"Let's pretend before you go," she breathed in his ear.
"Pretend there's a great big mistletoe hanging from the
ceiling."

"Please, Joy, I—"

She cut him off with a long hot kiss. He was a most
gracious recipient, kissing her back with skill and relish. But there was something missing. His touch. She
melted over his lap like a second skin, hoping to rest her
bottom in the breadth of his huge palm. But she
couldn't find his hands. They hadn't connected with her
body at all. "Hmm . . . Danny?" He opened his eyes in
heavy-lidded query. "Where are those magic fingers of
yours, baby?"

"The only place I can trust them," Dan uttered
against her lips. "On the table."

REX PULLED UP AT THE curb in the gold sedan a short
time later. Dan appeared on the sound of his third
honk, hustling down his front walk with his hair askew
and his topcoat slung over his arm.

"Dan Burke in a tizzy?" Rex needled mockingly as he
climbed into the car.

"No, just got off schedule with unexpected chores,"
Dan lied, twisting to toss the coat into the back seat.

"How long can it take to seal off a cellar, clean up a
few cookie crumbs?"

"Had to shovel the walk, too, inside and outside the
fence," Dan continued defensively, settling back with-

out meeting his partner's eyes. "It's a law, you know, shoveling the sidewalk. It's my duty to set an example."

Rex's eyes danced with mischief. "Jeepers, yeah."

"You just don't think about those things, with your apartment."

Dan busily gazed out the windshield as they rolled down their usual route toward the freeway, all the while aware of Rex's persistent scrutiny. "Is something wrong?"

"You've got a crazy bulge."

Dan's taut jaw slacked open. "I do not!" Not anymore, anyhow.

"It's right there," Rex persisted, "in your suit jacket."

Dan patted his pocket. Oh, yes. The breakfast-table lap trick. He reluctantly withdrew his cereal spoon, the one he'd smuggled away from Joy's prying eyes.

"Hey, you bent the thing in half!" Rex hooted in amazement. "Like Uri Geller on TV!"

Dan felt a flush rise from his neck as he mumbled something.

Rex gaped at him in boyish wonder. "What a remarkable feat. How'd you do it?" Dan heaved a laborious sigh. "I can only say, partner, that I had both hands on the table at the time."

DAN DIDN'T GET TO HIS personal errands until after hours. He had managed to locate Repeat with a few phone calls at lunchtime while Rex was out getting Chinese for the office. The informant had agreed to meet him at six-thirty at The Jigger, an unobtrusive neighborhood bar on University Avenue. Repeat often chose The Jigger for a meet and Dan suspected he lived in the area. But he never checked up on the hunch. It was part of their gentleman's agreement.

Dan was a little late as he pulled into the tiny lot adjacent to the ancient bar. He'd been obliged to take Rex home first, then race on to collect Joy's trunk.

Repeat was waiting for him inside at a table near the back—a nice secluded one with a view of the whole place. Dan nodded in recognition, pausing at the pay phone to call his own home and leave an estimated time of arrival for Joy. He ordered a ginger ale and a Scotch at the bar, then with glasses in hand, wound his way through the patrons.

"I wasn't going to wait for ya much longer," Repeat complained, greedily accepting the Scotch, pushing aside the one he'd been nursing to hold the table.

Dan settled back in a chair, taking a sip of ginger ale. "Busy day. People do crazy things around the holidays."

"They do crazy things all the time," Repeat snorted, as he pressed a cigarette between his lips. "Luckily the snitching business isn't seasonal."

"Yeah." Dan studied the little man in the woolen sports jacket who looked far older than his forty-odd years. He sported a couple of knife scars on his cheek and had a hairline that had seen denser days. His lips were too large for his narrow face and his teeth were yellowed and crooked. Dan accepted Repeat for what he was—a rough-hewn streetwise informant who did the right thing for a price. He considered himself a small business and Dan a good customer.

In general, Dan managed quite well on the streets. He kept his sources private and paid them well. Repeat in particular was a very reliable snitch. And he loved to talk. Sometimes Dan got a whole lot more than he paid for. Tonight, however, he was after only one thing. Then it was home to Joy's sweet company.

Dan inhaled shallowly in the cloud of smoke growing around them. All these little places smelled like cigarettes and stale beer. It seeped into the cheap paneling and flooring, fusing forever more into the decor.

"So what's got you all worked up?" Repeat demanded impatiently.

Dan knew his pride was a bit bruised. Repeat liked to be on top of everything, to call the shots and impress Dan with his up-to-date information. His irritation was a bad sign. If Repeat had anything current on the Jerome Berkley scam, he'd probably be wearing a knowing smirk, answering Dan's questions before he asked them. Dan hated to express initial interest, fearful of tipping someone off about Joy's return. But Repeat had never betrayed him—yet. He steepled his hands around his frosted glass, intent on keeping his tone smooth. "Anything on the vine about Jerome Berkley lately?"

"Say what?" Repeat hooted, striking a match to another cigarette.

"You think the whole mess is dead and buried for good?" Dan prodded.

Repeat raised his eyes to the ceiling. "It was dead and buried."

Dan's head shot up from his drink. "Hear of a loose end?"

"Hell, no!" Repeat drained his glass and Dan signaled the waitress.

"Then what do you mean?"

"I mean the book." Repeat had a high-pitched giggle that wasn't especially flattering. "That prosecutor, William Harris, the one who put Lieutenant Berkley away. He's writing a book about the trial." Repeat squinted in the haze of his own smoke. "Didn't you know? Isn't your sister still dating that jerk?"

"Yeah, she's still dating that jerk." Dan's features narrowed. "What about this book deal?"

"Hell, I figured you knew. Got it straight from Theo Nelson up at the Stillwater pen, myself. I stop by there to see him a couple times a month. Half his two-year sentence is over. Anyways, Harris expected to hit it big for the work he done on the case," Repeat went on to explain. "Wants to move into private practice and become one of those celebrity lawyers. Wants to be on Donyhue and Opry. The sap."

Dan's temper boiled. William Harris had been more concerned about the part in his hair than he'd been about his part in the case. The work of Harris's staff, and Joy's testimony had gotten him the conviction.

"Harris has been to see Theo twice. Guess he figures Theo, being the owner of the Laff Trak, has the inside scoop on how Berkley's money-laundering scam worked." Repeat's head dipped to meet his drink halfway. "Lieutenant Berkley sure the hell isn't going to help William Harris out. All he wants is for the world to forget he's a murdering louse."

"Theo Nelson cooperating?"

"Not yet. And don't ask me why he's stalling. Maybe he likes to jerk Harris's chain. You know, get his hopes up for nothin'."

"Does sound fun," Dan muttered, thinking how amusing it would be to jerk Harris's chain himself. He and the prosecutor frequently butted heads, over Dan's refusal to slant his testimony toward state's evidence. It was Dan's policy to testify objectively. "So, is that all you got?"

Repeat flashed tobacco-yellow teeth. "Whaddaya want?"

"To know if it's really all over."

"The Jerome Berkley murder trial?" Repeat reared in surprise. "Sure, it is. With all the players rounded up and Theo's comedy club out of business, there's nothing left to chew on. Ratting on Berkley really was a good deal for Theo." Repeat blew smoke from his nostrils, flicking the burning tip of his cigarette into a heaping tin ashtray at his elbow. "He got a light sentence, and will have another chance. I don't think he meant to get involved in the murder. He's just a small-time bumbler who let Berkley work out of his club. Sometimes a guy has to cut corners, ya know?"

Dan's doubts about Theo Nelson would forever waver in his mind. The three-hundred-pound hulk liked to come off as an unlucky bumbler, but forcing Joy into that getaway chase with him had been a cruel thing to do to a loyal friend and employee.

"Sometimes I still wonder about the money Berkley passed to Theo before the murder," Repeat muttered in thought. "You know, the payment for the false alibi. Joy Jones didn't dream up that envelope. Of course, Theo still says there was no dough. But the dumb schmuck did have a week to stash it someplace."

"Never did turn up," Dan conceded levelly. He drained his glass of ginger ale. "Guess I'll be shoving off." Dan reached into his coat for his gloves, unobtrusively pulling a folded bill out of the left thumb. He slid it under the ashtray as he got to his feet. "Let me know if anything heats up."

Repeat transferred the money to his cigarette pack. "You're the first one I'll call."

"And the last."

Repeat glanced at the number on the bill. "At these prices, you bet."

5

Here comes Scrooge

IT WAS NEARLY EIGHT o'clock when Dan rolled on to Pendham Avenue. All seemed secure as he eased the gold sedan up to the bank of mailboxes positioned on his boulevard. The shades were still drawn against the front windows, giving his regal gray castle a normal facade amid the gaily decorated homes. Home sweet perfect.

Dan emerged from the unmarked city vehicle, stepping into the beam of his own headlights to unlock his box and collect his mail. A breath of relief escaped his lips. Relief that the house remained standing?

So what had he expected her to do, anyway? Strike up a six-piece band and march the length of the avenue banging cymbals to the beat of "Jingle Bells"?

Maybe he should have given her the benefit of a doubt, entrusted her with the house keys she so wanted.

Too risky, he nixed. House keys would have led to mailbox keys, which would have led to car keys. He couldn't have functioned, knowing that she could scamper out to the street and gather the Christmas cards from his box, or fire up his black two-door Saturn automobile, presently parked in the garage out back off the alley. These temptations would have been far too great for the irrepressible nymph.

Though poetry in motion, Joy was literally always in motion. A trait that enchanted him and frightened him at the same time. It was so difficult to believe she desired him. He was just a regular, methodical guy who thrived on routine.

So what was the draw?

Maybe it was simply his skills as a lover she wanted. He shook his head, drawing a dry, private smile in the night. His ego ate that one up. But his heart wasn't so impressed. And his heart was involved. Her Christmas card had unglued him, dredging up some very foreign emotions. Emotions at war with each other. Anger. Relief. Elation. Frustration. He was utterly confused in his feelings for her. Had there been more to their fling than he realized? Was he enamored with the fantasy or with the woman? He wanted to be with her all the time. Even though it was torture not to really touch her, he couldn't wait to get close enough to be tempted all over again!

Dan rounded the mailbox on the boulevard and inserted his key in door number 3. It was a community box serving nine addresses. A decade ago the mailman came up the steps and shoved the mail through a slot in the door. The good old days.

He'd just grabbed his mail when he caught sight of the very pregnant Jane Weaver across the avenue. She was stepping off the curb and into the street like a slow majestic ship, her cloth coat draped open at the sides of her swollen belly. No one ever deliberately bothered this old Scrooge face-to-face. So why—

Panic jolted him. She must be in labor! Nothing short of an emergency could provoke her into a one-on-one collision—uh, meeting. Dan had much compassion for mothers-to-be in general. He'd even delivered a couple of babies over the years while on duty in a black-and-white. But a second damsel in distress showing up on sedate Pendham Avenue in a twenty-four-hour period seemed unbelievable. Rex would have a field day with this, if he got wind of it.

"Good evening, Detective Burke."

"Good evening, ma'am," Dan greeted, gripping his letters tighter. "Is everything all right?"

"Fine, just fine," she replied brightly.

Eye contact with a neighbor. He shifted from foot to foot, determined to hold her gaze as long as she wished. She didn't seem to be the least bit distraught, the least bit in pain. What did he see? Merry expectation?

"Is there anything I can do for you?" he asked gently.

"Why, no. Just thought I'd say Happy Holidays."

"Oh. Well. Same to you. Can I get your mail?" he added gallantly, extending his palm for her key.

"Heavens, no!" she declined with a laugh. "I retrieved it a while back. That's when I found out—" she wrinkled her nose "—you know."

"I do?"

A maroon van belonging to the family two doors down rolled by, giving a toot to its horn. It stopped at the box and the driver's window zipped down. "Evenin' there, Detective! Jane." It was George Maynard, the thirty-eight-year-old lawyer who Mrs. Nettel said was hopelessly trying to master the saxophone.

"Good evening," Dan repeated, cutting a slit of a smile. Something was very wrong here. Dan had lived alone in his family home for years without these frivolous exchanges. What could have happened during a single day to tear away his protective shield? Make him approachable, delightful, and agonizingly irresistible to these strangers?

"Joy!" The lament leaped right out of his mouth into the chilly air.

"Joy?" George Maynard repeated blankly. "By golly, yes. Joy to you, too!" With another honk he was on his way.

Dan looked down again at Timmy's mother, Jane. "You were about to tell me something?" he prompted.

She reached out to pat his hand. She actually took his hand! "I just want you to know—we all want you to know—what a great thing it is you're doing for her."

"*Her?*"

"Don't be so modest." Her voice dropped to a conspiratorial note. "Mrs. Nettel told us you were collecting for a clothing drive for the missions. But to take in the missionary herself for the holidays is so kind of you!"

Waiting for her to release his hand was one of the longest moments of his life. "I really must go inside now," he said tightly.

"Oh, yes," she gushed with a nod. "Enjoy your surprise."

There was more? Dan rattled off a silent count to ninety-seven as he waited for Jane Weaver to steer herself and her precious cargo back across the street and into her house. He dove behind the wheel with 911 urgency and took the sedan down to the corner and back around to the alley flanking the backyards. He swung into his shallow driveway, stopping short at the door of his ancient garage.

He could see it all under the glare of his own yard-security lights.

Movement—gliding and colorful.

Inside his fence.

Hooting, shouting, laughing.

On the inside.

Little miniature people, surrounded by one larger miniature person.

His precious sanctuary was under siege!

Dan marched to the gaping back gate, his topcoat billowing behind him like a villainous cloak. What was going on? He looked through the haze of his fury and alarm to focus on the activity.

The natural pond in the center of his spacious backyard had been shoveled clean and the ice was alive with skaters. Joy was in the center of it all, her tiny feet encased in his sister Gwen's old red-and-white Minnie Mouse skates. She wore old clothing, no doubt from his charity drive: a blue corduroy coat with a hood tied very snugly around her head and baggy brown pants that whipped around her legs as she skimmed gracefully across the ice. Youngsters zipped and yipped in gleeful pandemonium.

The scene took him back to when he and Gwen used to do the same thing. Especially around Christmas when his father, the Senator, wished to make a big splash with his friends, inviting them all over with their children for hot cocoa and skating. It was okay to let go then. The Senator had wanted them to come alive then. Just like windup toys. But ultimately the party ended, the guests and the press went home. He and Gwen were left in a hollow house, pretending that the sham of a celebration had been the real thing.

No one outside their home knew the real Marcus Burke or his sophisticated wife, Beth. The constituents loved their dapper, distinguished Senator and his chic helpmate. They faced the public with clear shining eyes, pushing forth their two apple-cheeked children. He and Gwen learned to perform in public early on. Why, it was the only time either of their parents ever embraced them, fussed over them, or beamed at them in admiration. Behind closed doors Gwen, four years his senior, took him in tow, playing mother, sister, friend. They weren't allowed outside the yard to play. What if they offended a neighbor, broke a window, trampled a garden?

Watching children at play always triggered these painful flashbacks. But Christmas was the worst. All those years, locked away with staff while his parents frolicked around town. Knowing that up and down the street other children were laughing inside those decorated houses. Of course, their house had been lit up back then; hundreds of lights in a rainbow of color blinked into the night with a phony message of goodwill. That was why he couldn't tolerate decorating the house himself. There still was no warmth inside to make it honest.

He'd had a flicker of hope last year with Joy. He'd thought if he pretended the house had spirit, they could make the image come true. But of course all that hope had vanished when she did.

Yes, she was back. And at his most vulnerable time of year. But he was going to tread with extreme caution. He would go on with his safe traditions and give her the chance to share them. But he wouldn't stick his neck out as he'd planned to last year. The turn in the case and her subsequent flight had nearly destroyed him. This Christmas offered no better guarantees. She was as unpredictable as ever and in at least as much danger.

Dan didn't know how long he'd been immersed in his bittersweet thoughts, a rigid dark figure lost somewhere in time. But suddenly the name "Scrooge" bellowed across the yard. Children were plunging into snowbanks, yanking off skates, pulling on boots. They hopped back to their feet with youthful energy, rounding the front of the house as fast as their legs would carry them.

The ice was clear, except for Joy, who skated on in whimsical rebellion; and one little stray who had taken a fall in the ruckus.

Dan crossed the ice to the boy, his shoes making an echoing thump in the quiet night air. "Steady, there..." Dan looked down at the upturned face, a freckled complexion red from the wind, eyes bulging in fear. "Steady, Jeremy."

"How'd ya know my name? I ain't done nothin'!"

"I know everybody's name," Dan answered in surprise. "Policemen are very good at remembering details."

"Don't arrest me, sir!"

Dan winced as Jeremy shrank from his helping hand. This kid was scared to death of him! And he knew exactly how he felt, just as though the autocratical Senator were standing over him at that age. For the first time the effects of his Dirty Harry image in the neighborhood hit home. He didn't wanted to be feared by this child, or any other. After living in a cloud of trepidation himself, it horrified him to think he could incite such panic in anyone else.

"Jeremy, I'm not going to arrest you."

"You hate us kids," he wailed in accusation. "You want us in jail!"

Jeremy looked at Joy, who had deliberately skated to the far side of the pond. Dan noted her slackened jaw, however. She couldn't believe this scene. Would she hate him?

"I don't feel that way at all," Dan hurriedly denied. A silence fell over the night. He dropped to his knee on the ice. "Look here," he said evenly. "I could never, ever hate a child. I just have a very stressful job and at night I need rest, quiet time to relax."

"Oh." Jeremy sniffed.

Dan dug into his coat for a tissue and held it to the boy's runny nose. "Blow. Again." Dan stuffed the tissue into the boy's pocket. Jeremy remained still with his eyes down, as if praying for his problem to vanish. "I'll bet your folks sometimes ask you to settle down and give them space, don't they?" Dan challenged softly.

When Jeremy lifted his eyes this time, they held more disappointment than fear. "Yeah, but you do it *all* the time."

"Guess it seems like I've forgotten how to be a kid, doesn't it?"

"Yeah," he agreed unmercifully.

"Well, I never got to be a kid, not like you are," Dan attempted to explain. "When I was your age, I had a lot of rules to follow. I lived right here, you know. I wasn't allowed to play with the guys in the street. I just had my sister most of the time."

"Your *sister*? Ick! No wonder you're a crabby old man."

Dan bit back a smile. "You have a sister, too, don't you?"

"Yeah, and she's darn bossy."

"Mine is, too. But she's pretty great. Likes to take care of me."

"How come they can be mean and nice together?" Jeremy asked earnestly, allowing Dan to hook a hand under his elbow and hoist him up on his blades.

Dan tipped his head down for a moment of male bonding. "Women are a mystery to us all, buddy. But we just can't seem to live without them." Dan straightened, noting that Joy had skated a little closer in an effort to eavesdrop.

"I'll tell you what," Dan proposed in a clearer tone. "What if I let you youngsters skate here at certain times?"

"Really, Detective?"

"You tell the others that we'll work something out." Dan guided him to the last pair of little boots in the snow. "But that means you'll respect my privacy at other times. When I'm busy or tired."

"All right, Detective Burke."

Dan helped him off with his skates. "Can you make it home?"

"Sure." Jeremy waved to the woman waiting on the stoop next door, then trotted for the back gate. "Night, Sister!" he called out to Joy.

"Good night, Jeremy," she returned cheerily.

"*Sister?*" Dan quietly growled, skimming across the ice in her direction. She tried to dodge him, but he caught her arm in a sure grip.

"Careful," she hissed. "You've got Mrs. Nettel peering out her window on one side and Jeremy and his mother on the other."

Dan didn't know exactly what character was lurking beneath Joy's hooded head. But he was going to put an end to this carnival here and now. "Your ankle, Sister!" he proclaimed in mock concern. "Of course I'll help you to the house!" With that he hoisted her atop his shoulder like a sack of flour.

"But my tennis shoes are back there!" she protested as he tipped her, bottom over teakettle. "Dan? Dan!"

Dan did something he'd never done before. He marched through his entire house in snow-covered shoes, oblivious to the trail of wet prints in his wake. He headed directly for the bedroom, depositing his parcel on the bed.

Joy bounced back on the mattress, her green eyes alight with mischief. "Ooh, Danny. How deliciously impetuous of you! Does this mean your control has snapped like the garter belt I might have on under these secondhand pants?"

"There is no garter belt under there," he declared with certainty. He switched on the bedside lamp and sank onto the mattress beside her.

"Wanna make a bet, copper?" It was a bet she didn't mind losing and they both knew it. One hand on her zipper and she figured he'd be a goner. To her disappointment, he hovered over her in a moment of indecision, then loosened the hood tied snugly at her chin.

"I brought you up here only to avoid prying eyes." He peeled off her jacket to find a tight purple T-shirt tucked into the waistband of the baggy old brown pants. Her nipples were rock hard beneath the cotton fabric. He tore his eyes away from them with great reluctance. "Didn't I tell you to stay inside?"

"I needed some fresh air around five, so I wandered out back," she explained without a trace of remorse. "Then I noticed patches of the pond beneath the snow. Then I thought of the skates up in Gwen's closet. Then I started shoveling."

"Then children started infiltrating my fence," he deduced, rubbing his temples. The woman was a virtual people magnet!

"Have you ever considered taking that yucky thing down?" she asked. "Gee, the kids weren't sure they even could come in your yard! And why did they call you Scrooge and blast off like that?"

"I have some public-relations trouble here on Pendham," he confessed. "Guess I just didn't realize how bad it was until tonight. It just so happens I need my peace and quiet, Joy. I very foolishly never figured it hurt anyone else."

"And why don't you have your lights on the house?" she probed. "You described them so vividly last year!"

He'd described the lights of his childhood. In an all-out effort to please her with a flawless holiday picture, he'd tossed them in. "Rex has had the lights all along," he hastened to assure. "Things got rather confused after you vanished, and we never strung them." No reason to tell her they were brand-new lights, bought last year at the last minute for the sole purpose of making their mutual Christmas fantasy come true.

"Well, let's go get those twinklers, mister!"

Dan balked at her impetuousness. "You're hiding out here, remember? Which means keeping a low profile through the holidays. No one is expecting lights to go up anymore."

Joy nibbled on her lip in contemplation. "You're right. As it is, I'm sure my arrival alone will be enough to keep the neighbors entertained."

Dan pulled a mirthless grin. "Just who the hell do my neighbors think you are?"

Joy's wind-flushed face lit up. "It's a doozy of a tale, let me tell you." She struggled to rise on her elbows as he set her tiny feet in his lap to unlace her skates. "Hope you did right...."

"*I* did right?" he repeated lethally.

"Could be wrong," she said with a philosophical sigh, "but don't be too hard on yourself."

"I wasn't consulted, Joy!" he roared, fumbling as his fingers became tangled in the red shoestrings.

"This was your brainstorm, copper. You told me to go through those boxes of used clothing, didn't you?" She fluttered her mittened hand. "Well, you know what an imagination I have. Naturally, when I came across those old habits, I was inspired."

Dan closed his eyes for a moment to absorb the news. "The new character for your repertoire is a nun."

"Exactly. Oh, it felt so good to sharpen my comedic skills on a whole new persona. I needed a new challenge, instant response from a fresh audience." Joy sat up, shaking her thick yellow hair loose on her shoulders. "Kids are the best, you know? So spontaneous, so honest. With their feelings always on tap just beneath a thin skin."

"Sounds like you."

"Guess so," she relented, tugging at her mittens. "Can't you see the beauty of it? An innocent nun whom you've taken in for the holidays. Everyone knows you've been collecting for some mission. Well, I gave the mission a name, and an ambassador. Goodwill Missions Worldwide, Sister Constance Clarence at your service. A charitable troubleshooter, if you will." She regarded him earnestly. "You see, Dan, the most believable lies are the simplest ones."

"I've told more lies in the past twenty-four hours than I've told in the last year." Dan eased the skates off and set them on the floor. "And somehow none of it seems the least bit simple to me."

"Mmm . . ." she purred. "Feels good."

Dan's features narrowed in perplexity. "What feels good?"

"My toes. You're rubbing them."

"So I am," he conceded, gazing down at the small stockinged feet in his hands.

"I managed to change my face just enough for dusk with the help of Gwen's makeup case," Joy chirped on, wiggling her toes.

Dan studied her face. Joy was undeniably a magician when it came to stepping into character. Her pale brows were etched into wide dark arcs. Her lashes were mascaraed, not for length but for color. Her pouty lips were narrowed down with a flesh-tone cover. Even her complexion was whiter than normal.

"Of course, with the stuff in my trunk, I could really transform myself."

"Well, I got the trunk," Dan announced, and was instantly rewarded with her delighted squeal. He felt a jolt of delight himself as she plunged into his lap. It felt so damn good to hold her, to bury his face in her fragrant hair. A man could get lost in Joy so easily, drown in her softness. . . .

"You're going to befriend those children, aren't you, Danny?" she asked, burrowing into his lapel. "Offering your ice rink will be the perfect icebreaker."

"Joy, as much as I'm willing to give it a test run with the pond, the timing couldn't be worse." Cupping her chin, he looked hard into her eyes. "The last thing you want to do is draw children into the yard with your life in jeopardy."

"I'm in disguise."

"You were in disguise in Orlando, too," he reminded.

"You're right," she admitted. "But I feel so safe here with you. And that problem seems so far away now." She punched the pillow at her side. "It's so hard to accept that I have an enemy at Christmas."

"I won't allow anyone to harm you," he consoled, patting her knee. "And I must admit your choice of disguise is shrewd. The Sister is a believable houseguest." He exhaled with a frown. "But please, no more surprises. You know I like to calculate things in advance."

"Same old cop. One minute you seem crazy about me, the next you seem determined to show me the door!"

"It seems to me you showed yourself the door last time," he bluntly corrected. "Something I can't handle a second time, Joy."

Joy's heart swelled with pleasure. He seemed so close to plunging into new, uncharted territory with her. "Danny, if you could just learn to be a little more flexible in all things, I think you'd be a lot more content."

"Isn't guarding your body enough?"

"No. I want a little of your confidence, too. I knew the nun would work. Please cut me some slack, make me a real part of this team you say we have."

Before he could reply, the peal of the doorbell cut through the house.

"Dammit!" He tossed Joy off his lap reflexively, tensed and on the alert. "Sit tight. I'll be right back."

"Control freak!"

Mrs. Nettel was standing at the back door, her head of gray curls bobbing into view between the chiffon curtains she herself had sewn for the pane. At the sight of Dan, she lifted Joy's grungy tennis shoes into view.

If only he'd scooped them up along with his good-will missionary! But knowing the protective Mrs. N., she'd undoubtedly have found another excuse for this visit. It was so like her to clock his every move. Naturally she'd be more than curious about his new guest.

"Hello, Dan." She stepped over the threshold the moment he tugged open the door. "Sister Constance Clarence left these in the snowbank, and I didn't want them to end up buried out there."

"Thanks." Dan took the shoes and set them on the rug behind the door. "Sister hurt her ankle and needed some swift assistance."

The pleasant, plump woman frowned in concern. "Ah, is she all right, then?"

"Nothing serious, really." Dan rocked on his heels, impatient for her exit. Unfortunately Mrs. Nettel didn't share his sense of urgency. She slipped off her own boots and pattered over to the sink to polish her foggy spectacles with a dish towel. Dan felt ill at ease with her for the first time in their year-long friendship. He had no choice but to suspect her of involvement in Joy's predicament. And he was unsure what Joy might have told her in the form of explanation. Perhaps if he just let her chatter on in the way so natural to her . . .

"I hope you don't mind about the ice rink, Dan," she said, pulling up a chair at the table.

"It'll take some getting used to."

Mrs. Nettel shrugged with a puzzled gleam in her pale blue eyes. "The nun attracts kids like flies, she does. Never seen anything like it."

Dan rested his hip against the counter, folding his arms across his chest. He was so damn tired and hungry. But if Mrs. Nettel even suspected the latter, she'd whip up a meal fit for a king. And linger for another hour. "She tell you she's a goodwill ambassador?"

"She did," Mrs. Nettel affirmed, popping her glasses back on her nose. "Goodwill Missions Worldwide. Never heard of them. So many charities these days."

"I was happy to take her in for the holidays."

"You are the best," Mrs. Nettel assured warmly, reaching across the tabletop to center the salt-and-pepper shakers beside the napkin holder. "A gentleman best suited to protect."

Lord knows, he tried!

"Sounds like Sister Constance Clarence has quite a colorful background," Mrs. Nettel ventured, her face ripe with curiosity.

Dan's regarded her sharply. "Oh?"

"She calls herself the cutest name. It's right on the tip of my tongue. . . ."

He met her expectant look with Jeopardy-style pressure. "Charitable troubleshooter!" he blurted out a bit more triumphantly than he meant to.

"Yes, indeed!" she exclaimed, smacking the table.

"Why, hello, Mrs. N."

Dan whirled at the sound of Joy's voice. The show-biz ham would have to get in on the deception. And she would be already calling Mrs. Nettel by the more intimate "Mrs. N.," as all the other neighbors did.

Mrs. Nettel raised a challenging brow. "Should you be on your feet, Sister?"

Joy's bright eyes lit with fake bravado. "I'm fine, truly, I am."

Dan watched in fascination as Joy limped into the room dressed in a nun's habit. The transformation was spectacular. With her hair tucked under a flowing black veil and her makeup freshened, she did look altogether different. And domestic, he judged, skimming her inflated figure in the full-skirted ankle-length dress. Her breasts and hips had grown three times in size with the aid of some padding. The image was charming and deceptive.

"I haven't seen a nun in an old-fashioned habit like yours in years," Mrs. Nettel remarked.

"We are a humble order," Joy confessed meekly, clasping her hands somewhere beneath her sagging bogus bustline.

Mrs. Nettel nodded smugly. "Thought as much, m'dear."

"Did Dan tell you yet, Mrs. N.?" Joy asked steering her form carefully into a chair.

"Tell me what, Sister?"

Dan shot Joy a wary look. She glared at him. She was again chastising him for his lack of confidence. And she was right. Joy was a master at improvisation. She knew what to do when the spotlight hit her. "I haven't had a chance to tell Mrs. Nettel anything," he reported on a note of invitation.

Joy folded her hands on the table, addressing the other woman solemnly. "We must ask a favor of you, Mrs. Nettel. After all, you are a leader on the avenue."

Her lined face beamed. "I am?"

"Of course," Joy intoned. "Though my ankle is all right for walking, I really cannot skate on it for a while. Probably not until after Christmas."

"Lands," Mrs. Nettel tsked. "Perhaps you should see a doctor."

Joy raised a palm. "An unnecessary measure. I am hoping, however, that you can explain this to the children for us. It's just a temporary ban on the pond. I couldn't bear to watch them skate on without me."

Mrs. Nettel nodded her head. "Leave it to me, Sister. Dan will tell you I take quite good care of him around here."

"She does," he said, jumping in on cue. "Another big sister."

"A mother, surely," Mrs. Nettel chittered, openly flattered.

"Well, thank you for welcoming Sister to the neighborhood, Mrs. N.," Dan said with hints of farewell.

"My pleasure." Mrs. Nettel rose to her feet. "I can rest easy with my knitting tonight, knowing that Sister is fit. Until Saturday, then. I'll clean the house top to bottom for your Sunday do."

"Wonderful," Dan intoned, following her to the door. "I'll be at work, but Sister will be here to deal with the decorator delivering the tree."

"How can you work Saturday, with Christmas on Tuesday?" Joy demanded, dropping the dignity the moment Dan scooted Mrs. Nettel out the door.

"Joy, I always work a lot around Christmas. I think it unwise to bail out now. And I do have a mountain of paperwork to finish. For some mysterious reason, my concentration has been way off today."

"Oh, phooey!"

"Let's go out and get your trunk," he proposed in consolation. "Then you'll have your most precious possessions to paw through while I'm away."

Joy grinned begrudgingly. "Okay."

Dan held out his arm. "Well then, Sister, get a limp on."

JOY DELIBERATELY WAITED until later on in bed to talk to him about Mrs. Nettel. He was dozing off beside her in an appealingly woozy state—a little rumpled, a little tousled, but generally at peace. Dan had insisted upon being close all night long, but had asked her to stay on her own pillow, on her own side of the bed, to keep temptation to a minimum. Joy reluctantly complied because she understood how much it meant to him, that he wouldn't sleep a wink unless she was under his immediate care.

"Danny?"

He rolled over with a mumble. "Yeah, honey."

"You awake?"

"Sort of. Can't stop thinking about your new boobs."

"Just a secondhand bra and a couple grapefruits is all," she replied softly.

Dan yawned hugely. "That should break the spell."

"It must be really hard on you," she pressed ahead as

his face fell tranquil once more. "Suspecting your best people of betrayal, I mean."

"Yeah, it is."

Joy nibbled nervously at the maroon cuff of her sweatshirt sleeper. "You're, ah, really fond of Mrs. Nettel, aren't you?"

"Very fond . . . her . . ."

"But in a way, her fall would be the easiest to accept, I suppose."

Dan cracked an eye open. "You like her, too. I could tell."

Joy smiled tenderly. "I do like her. But of the three suspects—"

"This isn't a cheap Charlie Chan movie, Joy," he protested with a slight rise in his voice. "It hurts too much to call them suspects. Rex is like a brother, and Gwen is a sister. Both are pesty and opinionated. But they are family. So is Mrs. Nettel. She fusses over me the way my own mother never did. I am determined to give her and the others the benefit of the doubt until proven otherwise."

"There must be a way to figure out who's guilty."

"These things take time. And I told you all about Repeat's report while you rummaged through your trunk, didn't I?"

"How can William Harris's book be a tie-in?"

"Might not mean a thing," he grumbled, twisting on the mattress. "But you can't reveal yourself to him, either, until we know for sure. You'll have to be extremely cautious at the party."

"I get to go?" she rejoiced.

"Could I have stopped you?"

"No, but this invitation is so sweet." She leaned over and kissed his bristled cheek.

"Go to sleep, honey, and leave the spying and prying to me."

Joy watched him close his eyes again and drift back off. How touching that he considered her the only one who functioned on ninety-proof emotion. Though he'd never admit it even to himself, his sensitivity to the key players in this case made it unlikely that he could solve it on his own. He was going to need some help with the nitty-gritty.

She could step in now, disguised as Sister Constance Clarence, ambassador of the Goodwill Missions Worldwide. The first job would be to keep an eye on this maternal neighbor, Mrs. Nettel. Get to the bottom of her game.

Yes, as soon as she had some answers, she'd tell Dan. Tell him that Mrs. Nettel had been to the Laff Trak Comedy Club on more than one occasion during Joy's two-year stint there. Had had private meetings in Theo Nelson's office, meetings that left the dear Mrs. Nettel in a snit nearly every time.

A tough secret to keep. But Joy just couldn't add to his burden tonight. A man could only take so much. Hopefully, Mrs. Nettel was as harmless as she appeared.

6

Visions of sugar cookies

"SO HERE YOU ARE!" Gwen Burke opened the door to the interrogation room at the Metro Station the following afternoon to find Dan seated at a varnished wooden table, digging his lunch out of a deli sack.

"I left word for you at the front desk," he said, unwrapping a huge submarine sandwich.

Gwen looked smart in a skirted teal suit, her black hair pulled back in a smooth knot. She was a statuesque beauty of five foot eight, with Dan's sharp features and navy blue eyes. As Dan was a methodical policeman, his sister was a methodical accountant. She worked for a large firm several blocks away on Cedar.

"Dining in an interrogation room?" She balked in disapproval. "Really, Dan."

"It's officially known as the interviewing room these days," he corrected. "And the perfect place for some quiet time." With a boyish grin he offered her half his sandwich.

Gwen moved over to the table to peek inside the bun. "Ham, salami, and three different cheeses?"

"Plus shredded lettuce and tomato."

"You're on."

Gwen pulled up a chair as Dan ripped the wrapper down the center and slid her share of the enormous sub across the table.

"I stopped by your office first," she remarked, picking at the overflowing shreds of lettuce. "Rex was on the telephone. He cut short the call, let me tell you. Made me feel as welcome as the plague."

"Really?" Dan produced three milk cartons, pushing one toward her. "He said he needed some privacy, but it's not like him to keep secrets."

"You fellows have a spat?"

"No, no, of course not," Dan honestly assured. "What exactly happened?"

"Well, at first he was reaming somebody over the wire about how loyalties can be complicated. Then he hung up with a slam and said you were in here. I explained that I thought there'd been a mistake. I lingered for a minute, bringing up the fun we three had at our Saturday spritz bake-off. He was slamming drawers open and shut, as if I didn't matter a whit. Then I made an innocent remark about his new watch. He got positively crazed. Said he never should've worn it to work. Then he ordered me out!"

"Gwen, why did you notice his watch, of all things?"

"Because it's a Rolex!"

"He didn't have it yesterday," Dan remembered.

"I can't believe he has it now! You and I have them because we inherited scads of money, but Rex..." Gwen shrugged helplessly. "I thought he was from a humble home."

"You're sure about the quality, Gwen?"

Gwen nibbled at her bun with a wry look. "I know a Rolex, brother dear. The hands sweep fluidly over the numbers like no imitation's ever could. Odd, too, how angry the question made him. An absolute brute, he was."

Dan's brows drew together in sharp black slashes. "It certainly doesn't jibe with his modest life-style—the mid-scale car and the one-bedroom apartment."

Gwen rolled her eyes. "The loud clothing and the water bed."

Rex avoided personal reminiscences and Dan never pried. Rex's parents lived out west someplace, and his brother in New England. There was never any color added to the picture. "He's never flashed anything tasteful at us before, has he?" Dan pondered.

"Heavens, no!" She swiveled in her chair, eyes searching the stark room. "Any cups in here?"

"Just straws." When she scowled in distaste, he chuckled as a snide younger sibling should. "Get common just this once. Many a stakeout I'd kill for one."

Gwen poked the straw into the carton with a confused shake of her head. "I've never seen the cad with a huge amount of cash, or in a tempestuous fit, either. So what gives?"

Dan munched on his sandwich. "The watch could be a gift from one of those babes he keeps on tap. The flare-up could be from the same source."

"Be sure to keep me posted. I'm dying of curiosity."

"He'll be at the party," Dan reminded her.

"With an apology if he's wise," she grumbled. With a glance at her own elegant diamond-studded time-piece, she asked the obvious: "So, why did you want to see me?"

"To play catch-up with my sister. Recap party plans." It was the truth, up to a point. He wanted to grill her about the Christmas card, and perhaps sway her on the subject of the lover-boy prosecutor she was so enamored with. He squeezed his eyes shut for a moment. Even Repeat knew that William Harris had his fangs in his sister. How could such a levelheaded woman, a hardheaded woman, end up with that slick opportunist?

"I've gotten several prominent out-of-town responses," Gwen said excitedly. "The Winstons and the Prestons. The Calhouns."

"Glad to hear it."

Gwen peered across the table at him with an anxious eye. "You are looking forward to the party, aren't you, Dan?"

"It's tradition," he replied simply, stabbing his straw into a second carton of milk. "People count on coming. And it means a lot to you."

"It's supposed to help both of us fight off those lonely memories," Gwen cajoled.

Dan pinched his straw. "In the beginning, after the folks died, it was a helpful distraction. The high-powered crowd they exposed us to seemed like just the right kind of guest."

"And still are!" Gwen insisted in surprise. "Those ties mean so much to me."

Dan shrugged. "Rex suggested I invite our softball team this year."

"The water bed crowd? The beer-can bunch?"

"Oh, c'mon, Gwen!" Dan rolled his eyes. "You did ask for my opinion."

"You don't seem yourself at all," Gwen noted accusingly. "You've never considered mixing different classes of people in a social setting before. Never invited me to

lunch in such an odd setting, either—and at the last
minute, yet! Even your hair is parted farther to the left,"
she decided after close scrutiny.

Joy had messed with his hair at breakfast. He'd
messed with hers, too. They'd forgotten all about eating. "Maybe I'm trying to loosen up a little bit," he retorted.

"You love your routine," she argued in confusion.

"They are such little things," Dan said dismissively.
"Things you shouldn't even have noticed."

"See what I mean?" she challenged shrilly. "The old
you would've expected me to notice." She reached over
and grasped his hand. "I'm only asking because I'm
worried. If you are cracking up, I want to help."

"For Pete's sake!" He took his hand from hers with a
rap. "The only real issue here is the reception. It just
seems more like an unnecessary security blanket to me
these days. Why, last year, you had to prop me up
through the whole thing."

"Only because the Kodak Comic unceremoniously
dumped you," she declared flatly. "All she's managed
to leave you with is another blue Christmas memory.
And a very unfestive mood, by the looks of it."

"Her name is Joy. And my moods are not her fault."
All in all, his moods were to her credit, he privately
amended, his insides warming at the thought of her
kittenish playfulness. She was driving him delightfully
mad with her seductive ploys and spontaneous bursts
of energy. If he thought he could give in and still retain
his detective skills, he'd revisit heaven. As it was, control was still the priority of the hour. Boy, those hours
dragged on each night lying beside her in the same bed.

If she knew just how close he was to cracking, she'd snare him with the crook of a finger.

"You still with me, Dan?"

"Yes." With a determined tug back, he moved ahead with his plan. "Somebody took her Christmas card," he said, hoping to catch Gwen off guard.

"Joy's? Really?" Gwen didn't so much as flinch. "How odd."

"It meant a lot to me," he confessed.

"Take my advice, start fresh this Christmas. Find yourself a real live date for the party."

"You bringing a date?" Dan probed.

"Of course. William is escorting me." She tsked impatiently. "He's looking forward to it. Had such a good time last year."

"I hear he's writing a book on the Jerome Berkley murder trial," Dan reported, openly betrayed.

Gwen caught her breath. "I was going to tell you."

"I got it from a street informant." His dark eyes gleamed in displeasure.

"William's just getting his notes together, scheduling interviews."

"He's already conducting interviews," Dan corrected with a silent thanks to Repeat. "Paid two visits to Stillwater prison to see Theo Nelson, owner of the defunct Laff Trak Comedy Club."

Gwen sighed hard. "All right, yes. William is working diligently on the book. He predicted that you'd be annoyed and has been tiptoeing around you."

"Why would I be mad?" Dan wondered.

She compressed her lips, as if the injured party. "Professional jealousy. Resentment over him stealing me away."

"That's nonsense!" he growled. Did Harris truly believe those notions, or was he purposely causing a diversion to throw the scent off something else? This trick served Harris well in court.

"You'd think Theo Nelson would be too annoyed to contribute to the book," Dan pointed out logically. "Being locked up because of Harris and all."

"William cut him a generous deal for his cooperation," Gwen countered with obvious pride. "He'll be out in a year."

"Harris been edgy after his visits?"

Gwen's thin brows lifted in contemplation. "I suppose he was the first time. He was better the second time, though."

"When was that?"

"Last Saturday, I believe. The day we made the cookies. William and I had a late supper at my place. He . . . eventually relaxed. . . ." She trailed off, her complexion pink.

"He talk to anybody else?"

"He tried to contact Jerome Berkley in that out-of-state prison, but he doesn't want to see his case rehashed again," she reported, harmonizing with Repeat's version. "Wouldn't even speak to William."

"Wonder if he's chatted with Rex?"

Gwen's eyes widened in fear. "You think Rex's Rolex came from William, and that the loyalty thing on the phone today was about the Berkley case."

"I don't know, Gwen," he admitted quietly.

"It doesn't make sense."

Unless Harris hired Rex to track down Joy. Did he want her interview that badly? If so, why not just come out of hiding and ask for it? "Don't get all huffy," he placated. "I'm just sifting through the possibilities. He ever express interest in locating Joy?"

"Hasn't said a word to me," Gwen replied. "Would it be so wrong if he wanted to interview you and Joy if that were possible? Joy is safe now, isn't she?"

"I don't know," he said in all honesty.

"Of course you wouldn't," she murmured sympathetically. "With her on the run and all. Dan, what difference could it make to you if William writes this book, interviews half the world to do it?"

Joy was all the difference. Dan didn't give a rip about the book, or what Harris would ultimately get for it. But he couldn't tell Gwen that without tipping his hand.

"I hear he's leaving the D.A.'s office," he went on. "Going into private practice."

"He hopes to," she affirmed proudly. Then under his glower she added, "I wish you could approve of my choice of men. William is the one I want. He fits so well into our social circle. He has the polished graces and valuable connections I admire, that we grew up with."

Dan knew she was comparing Harris with Joy in a sneaky backhanded way. But Joy was real. Every ounce of her was genuine—except the occasional padding to round off a character. William Harris was always trying to cut corners to get his way.

"Tell you what, Gwen, if you stop harping on Joy, I'll lay off Harris for the holidays," Dan said.

Gwen patted his hand on the table. "It's a deal. And one in my favor," she gloated, "considering that you have to contend with William in person."

"Just call me Father Christmas, little girl," he said with a wink.

Gwen stood, the last of her sandwich wrapped neatly for travel. "Father Christmas," she echoed sweetly. "Is that what the Sister calls you?"

It was Dan's turn on the griddle; one so hot that he leaped up with a start.

"Sister Constance Clarence of the Goodwill Missions Worldwide," she rattled off with amazing tongue-twisting dexterity. "There's a whopper of a secret if I ever heard one."

Dan shoved his hands in his pockets and smirked. "Mrs. Nettel has been naughty, it seems."

"She has been a jewel!" Gwen proclaimed gratefully. "I called to confirm her help with Sunday night's meal and she told me all about your new houseguest." She sniffed in disappointment. "I was waiting for you to tell me about her."

"Guess we're even," he bartered with a grin. "Harris's book on Jerome Berkley and my houseguest, the good Sister."

"I hate secrets of all kinds."

"I was going to tell you about the nun, but I didn't want you trying to tinker with the arrangement."

"Me, tinker?" she gasped.

"You're the master!" He gave her shoulders a squeeze. "You think you know what's best for me always."

"And you for me!" she retorted ruefully, moving for the door.

"Sister Constance Clarence is just a dear wayward soul who had no place to stay. The mission knew I was collecting clothing for them and they contacted me, hoping I could find her shelter."

"But that was a different mission, as I recall," Gwen countered.

"You know how fast goodwill spreads," he improvised airily. "Mission to mission. Nun to nun."

Gwen had no reason to distrust her brother and therefore accepted his reasonable explanation. "I'm sure she'll be a gracious asset to the party," she assured with a hand on the doorknob. "By the way, did she sample my little spritz masterpieces?"

Did she!

"Didn't even think of it, did you?" she chided in erroneous assumption. "They would be just the treat with after-dinner coffee, artistically arranged on a dessert plate with some mint ice cream."

Dan felt a twinge of conscience over Joy's feast, and not for the first time. It was doubtful that she had acknowledged, on even the most superficial level, the painstaking detail given each and every cookie. From hand to mouth they had gone.

He'd have to set it right tonight, give Joy a look at the spritz from the other side of the oven.

"Well, I'm off," Gwen announced. "I'm going to take you at your word that you're all right. For now anyway. Oh, and thanks for lunch. The interrogative ambience was *magnifique*."

"Mind your own business through Christmas and I'll take you to brunch at Speare's," he tempted.

Gwen yanked open the door and to their mutual surprise, William Harris was on the other side. "Hello, darling!" he enthused with open-armed surprise.

"Hello, sweetie," Dan responded, smiling at the handsome prosecutor. There was no denying he was effective in court, with his schoolboy face, his brown head of hair styled short, his dark beard clipped square and neat. He was aging gracefully. Approximately Repeat's age, but in peak physical condition.

William embraced Gwen, eyeing Dan quizzically over her shoulder. "Roll out of the wrong side of the bed?"

"He knows about the book, William," Gwen murmured in his ear.

"Been meaning to tell you all about it," Harris assured heartily.

"Right," Dan agreed. "You looking for me?"

"I was. But the most lovely distraction has voided my mind," he claimed, with eyes only for Gwen.

Dan repressed the urge to retort a snide something.

"I'm due back at work," Gwen informed Harris endearingly.

Harris slid a hand around her waist. "I'll walk you to the street."

"I want to talk to you, William," Dan interceded on a threatening note.

"I was just coming to tell you I'm officially on vacation until after Christmas," Harris announced airily.

"About this book—"

"See you at your party," he called over his shoulder, tugging Gwen down the hall toward the bank of elevators.

Dan closed the door behind them, leaning against it for a moment of meditative review. Questioning a guy's own sister was no lark. But the talk had been quite fruitful. Gwen had no inkling of Joy's return and Rex the people pleaser was having a public-relations problem he didn't want to discuss. The painful news, however, was that Gwen was willing to keep secrets from him concerning William Harris. And that moony expression she reserved just for Harris was downright scary. She was capable of giving him Joy's Christmas card if she thought he could make use of it—if for example, he wished to track Joy down for the sake of his book. But could Gwen lie to Dan outright? Thinking back on their dialogue, Dan realized that she never really did deny taking the card. Not a good sign . . .

"ALL MY EXPERIENCE WITH cookies has been on the eating end, copper," Joy forewarned as Dan set two grocery bags on the kitchen table that evening.

"I figured as much." He swiveled on his heels to inspect her from head to toe. "A raw recruit if I ever saw one."

Joy flinched under his amorous scrutiny, looking down at her washed-out yellow sweatshirt and white slacks, straight out of a mission box. If he wanted her so badly, why didn't he just break down and take her?

"What are you grinning about?" she finally demanded, stepping up to rummage through the groceries.

"Just glad to be back here, I guess," he confessed, raking his fingers through her tide of blond hair. It looked butter yellow against her paler shirt. Despite it all, having Joy to come home to was amazingly comforting.

"I found a radio station that plays only Christmas tunes," she ventured in conversation, acutely aware of his touch at her throat.

He paused for a moment to absorb the rendition of a slow classic. "Puts me right in the spirit."

He kneaded her shoulders with his powerful hands, hovering over her like a comforting blanket. She felt utterly safe in his care. But as always, whenever he was too close, the "blanket" hummed with electricity, leaving her hot and bothered and wanting.

Joy's heart lurched as he gathered her close and glided across the brown linoleum. "What are you doing, Danny?"

"Unwinding."

Joy squealed in surprise as he flung her back in his arms, lingering overhead with sparkling blue eyes full of needs and promises—and lust. She licked her lips in invitation. Keeping her dipped nearly upside down, he covered her mouth with his.

Heat shot clear through Joy as he held her in a hip-lock, liplock embrace. She was quaking in her little tennis shoes when he righted her on the floor again. Breathlessly she draped her arms on his shoulders. They were still swaying, without their feet leaving the floor. "I needed this, Danny."

"I remember many of your needs. Even the small ones..." He trailed off, resting his chin on the top of her head. "I've been thinking about the holidays all afternoon, and I'm going to try to fulfill all your dreams if I can. Make this a nice Christmas for us. If I can..."

Joy blinked in confusion. Dan was surely an old hand at Christmas frolic with his family, wasn't he? "Of course you can! You're my salvation."

His kissed her forehead with a wry smile. "I sometimes wonder who is the lifesaver around here."

She stood on tiptoe to rake through his thick black hair, drawing strands to his forehead. It gave him a sexy vulnerable look that turned her knees to jelly. "So, now what?"

"Time to bake," he informed her with regret.

"I could get out of it by stripping off your clothes," she threatened with a tantalizing look. "Making love to you under the table like we did at the safe house."

Dan caught her wrist in midair and nipped at her knuckles. "You could, but you won't."

Her gem-green eyes gleamed in mischief. "Oh, yeah?"

"You ate Gwen's cookies, and you know it's only right to replace them."

"Oh, yeah," she repeated with far less vigor.

"So, did you get my message on the machine?"

She blinked in innocence. "You left a message?"

His face narrowed. "Yes. I asked you to pick up five times."

"Oh. Well, before you told me not to answer the phone," she claimed sweetly. "I thought maybe it was a test."

"But I did leave directions on the tape, didn't I?"

"Yeah. Imagine having a Christmas-cookie recipe memorized!" she marveled in suspect sincerity. "You'll be pleased to hear that I did as you asked." She went over to the refrigerator and swept open the door with a flourish.

Dan released an audible sigh of relief at the sight of his mother's old red ceramic bowl mounded with a thick, creamy spritz dough.

"Know why I did it?" she challenged.

"Not really," he admitted with a laugh.

"Because you trusted me with your ten-pound bag of sugar." Joy put her hands on her hips, lifting her chin in pride.

"Actually, I was putting my faith in Sister Constance Clarence," he teased, reaching inside the fridge for the bowl. When Joy began to protest, Dan pushed a fingerful of dough into her mouth. "Every good turn deserves a reward."

"Oh, yes . . ." Grasping his hand, she sucked his finger clean.

"I'm trying to teach you moderation in all things," he chastised huskily. "Now be a good girl and give my finger back."

Instead she sucked all the more, savoring the taste and texture of his roughened skin against her teeth, over her moist, sensitive tongue.

"C'mon, honey," he eventually pleaded. "We've got work to do."

Joy meekly accepted her fate, pulling hot pads out of the drawer. "You must really get a charge out of this, going to so much trouble."

"It's tradition," he explained. "Started the first Christmas after our parents died together in a chartered plane explosion. It was our way of holding it all together. The cookie production gave us focus. We talked about a lot of things that first time. Ironed out a lot of family baggage . . ." He sighed, taking the cookie gun out of a high cupboard. "We've just kept it up. Gwen has gotten quite good at it," he added with caution. "And takes it far more seriously than I do."

Joy examined all the different design disks for the barrel of the gun. "Gwen never did like me, did she?"

"Gwen is a know-it-all who frequently doesn't give people a fair chance," Dan honestly assessed. "She talked to you only twice during the trial and made some unfair assumptions. She is very proper and discreet, and viewed your openness and impetuousness as unsuitable." In all fairness, he added, "I believe her ultimate complaint is that you left me pretty messed up for the holidays."

"I'm sorry," she said softly. "But leaving was the right thing to do. Just as I hope returning is."

Dan watched her step up to preheat the oven in her loose comfortable clothing, as though she did it every day. He couldn't help imagining just what it would be like, having her to come home to, night after night. Dan wanted nothing more than to have a wife here to cook him dinner. But he doubted Joy would even want to be here for a dinner he cooked! He spent enough evenings in smoky joints on duty, to know that her comedy-club hangouts wouldn't be appealing to him on a regular basis.

"This is a dream come true," she murmured, invading his thoughts.

"Yeah," he agreed huskily.

"Christmas in your house," she went on. "This big warm palace of a place."

Dan's back stiffened. The Christmas farce. Her obsession with it distressed him. But it was his own fault for pretending in the first place. "Actually, this old barn is sort of drafty on nights like this," he said a bit awkwardly. "I'm going upstairs and change into my sweats. And I'll build us a fire in the living-room hearth."

Pausing only for a light dinner, they soon got the cookie assembly line rolling. Since Dan knew how to work the gun, he pressed the small, molded cookies onto the sheets. Joy took over with the decorative sprinkles, straining to recall just what those cookies looked like. Thank goodness she was known as nothing less than the Kodak Comic!

"So Rex joins in on this madness," Joy contemplated aloud as she worked.

"Seems to relish in it," Dan affirmed, whisking a fresh batch into the oven. "Always available year-round, too. Even for the Fourth of July." He frowned, thinking back to Gwen's observations earlier in the day concerning Rex's mood and his Rolex. "He's so unpredictable sometimes. A people person with only perfunctory contact with his own people."

"Sometimes when chicks are kicked out of the nest, they fly away to seek approval elsewhere," Joy speculated softly.

"Maybe. Though he speaks highly of his parents—when he does speak of them." Dan reloaded the cookie barrel, taking for granted the silence between them. When he did look up at Joy, he found her eyes were glistening.

"This chick knows from experience," she explained under his concerned scrutiny. "I lived in a crummy little boardinghouse with my mother until I was seventeen. Never did anything right in her eyes. She'd been in some sort of auto accident when I was a baby. Sued and got a sizable reward. Never worked again. Never ventured farther than the neighborhood bar on the corner."

"What happened to your father?" he asked quietly.

"Never knew the guy."

Joy stared blankly at the shaded window over the sink, as if trying to stare right through it. What she did see was her mother's face etched there—sullen, angry, disappointed. "We lived on that settlement money all those years, and any little bit I could scrape up. Then she met a creep. When he came to live with us there

wasn't room for me anymore. He wanted me to stay."
She rolled her eyes. "And Mom wanted me to leave—
blamed me for his desires. I flew out of there! Started
bartending in clubs around the Cities. Became known
for my comedic skills behind the bar, eventually making my way up onstage with some of my jokes. The rest
you already know." She turned back to face him. "So
you see, I wasn't scamming you about Christmas back
at the hotel last year. I could tell by your eyes that you
didn't believe me, and ever since, I've want to set the
record straight on it." With a limpid look she sagged
into his arms. "I've missed you so. I've never needed
anyone the way I need you right now. My hero, my
Santa."

Dan set his chin on the top of her head with a qua-
vering breath. This woman was constantly challenging him to look at who he was. Unfortunately he didn't
especially like who he was seeing right now. The sad
truth was that he was far more capable of being the hero
who saved her life, than being the Santa who gave her
a merry Christmas.

7

Rockin' around the Christmas tree

"HEY, SLEEPYHEAD."

Joy's eyes fluttered open Saturday morning at the sound of Dan's rich voice. Unfortunately he was no longer nestled at her side under the covers. Already in shirt and slacks, he was at the closet, carefully perusing the collection of ties neatly draped over a row of pegs. From a distance the strips of silk blended together like a drab seascape. How tough could the choice be?

"I hate leaving you on the weekend this way," he said, plucking out a fog-gray tie from the seemingly interchangeable lot.

"We were up so late last night," she said on a yawn.

Dan smiled faintly. "It was time well spent."

Joy hugged her knees to her chest, sighing in reminiscence. It had been cozy, intimate. Dan had really listened when she'd poured out her sordid past. And it hadn't offended him as she'd feared it might. It was a huge weight off her mind.

They'd talked on and on, going into the complexities of her present situation, the possible sources of danger. Dan was getting itchy for answers.

"So you plan to follow up some leads today." Her gaze traveled with him as he strode toward the mirror.

His reflection flashed with hope as he strung his tie through his shirt collar. "You haven't thought of anything new, have you?"

"I never forget in the first place, remember?"

"Just hoping for a break."

"I have been rehashing, though," Joy began slowly. "Is it possible that someone thinks I have the envelope of alibi money Jerome Berkley passed to Theo that night at the club?"

Dan frowned, approaching the bed. "I've considered that angle. Even Repeat mentioned it at the bar. It popped right into his head at the mention of the trial. Could be someone hoped to make some easy cash off you. I'll give Henry Sheldon a call from the office today, see if anyone's been lurking around your Orlando place."

Her eyes softened at the thought of her concerned friend. "Send my best."

"I will."

"If it is the money, William Harris certainly isn't our stalker," Joy reasoned suddenly, fully expecting the disgruntled look she received. Dan added the prosecutor to the circle of possible suspects because of his forthcoming book. Joy, like Gwen, had found Harris utterly charming. Dan asserted that Harris treated her well to get her testimony. Joy liked to think most people liked her for herself. And Dan couldn't put Harris in jail just because he dated his sister. Surely he hadn't expected to choose Mr. Right for Gwen!

"Mrs. Nettel's abrupt appearance next door after the trial has to be explored, too," Dan mused, easing into his suit jacket. "Rex voiced doubts months ago concerning her busybody ways. I turned a blind eye because she was so perfect for me. Now I'm beginning to wonder if she was too perfect on purpose, just to get close. Like the others, she could've slipped off to Orlando without my knowledge."

Joy was tempted to tell him about Mrs. Nettel being at Theo Nelson's Laff Trak Comedy Club. But he'd take over that part of the probe, too, leaving her completely out of it. And Theo was her territory; had been her friend once upon a time, giving her that all-important first big break at his club. If Mrs. Nettel was in cahoots with him, Joy felt she was more capable of proving it.

And Dan didn't need any more bad news. He was really on the ropes as it was. He clearly hated unfinished business. Especially this kind, which was keeping him from letting go, from making wild mindless love with her.

It was difficult to believe that Dan couldn't consummate and concentrate at the same time. But Joy realized that if he believed he couldn't, then he couldn't.

"Think you can handle your role today?" he double-checked, sitting on the edge of the bed to slip on his black wingtips.

The query rankled every professional bone in her body. And if it hadn't been for the solicitous look he wore with the question, Joy would've pelted him with pillows. Accepting his concern with the affection obviously intended, she crawled across the mattress behind him, winding her arms around his neck.

"Please don't worry about me, copper," she murmured in the curve of his ear. "My metamorphosis into Sister Constance Clarence is downright astounding!

Just to add an extra dash of piety, I plan to dig some clear wire-rimmed lenses out of my trunk."

"If all goes well, we'll have you out of that habit in a day or two."

She was counting on it. If fear didn't cause her collapse, abstinence surely would! "Mrs. Nettel will be here soon," Dan noted with a glance at the clock. "Need help hauling your stuff across the hall to the guest room?"

"No, you go ahead," she assured, hopping off the bed. "I'm just going to slip into some clothes and get to work."

Dan's eyes moved with her. "Don't forget about the bust."

"The what!" she gasped incredulously.

"The wig on the bust," he clarified with an uncomfortable cough. "Shakespeare's bust."

"Better get outta here, copper," she shooed. "While you can!"

Dan did so. In a hotfooted hurry.

JUST AS DAN CLAIMED, Mrs. Nettel seemed to have no key of her own. Joy had just donned her habit and spectacles when the back doorbell rang.

"Hello, Mrs. Nettel!" Joy greeted, opening the door wide.

Mrs. Nettel bustled in with a nod of her curly gray head. "So glad to have your company, Sister. Dan is usually here on Saturdays, and we chat up a storm while I work."

Joy couldn't help musing that Mrs. Nettel certainly had woven her way into the fabric of Dan's life. And he being so solitary, it had no doubt been a cinch. All the more reason she should be the one to question her.

Of course, his instructions had been quite different. Joy was to stay in the background, say as little as possible, and help supervise the arrival of the department-store decorator with the crummy manicured tree. She couldn't afford to waste precious time playing it *that* safe.

"I'm just going to see if Dan has any mending up in the sewing room," Mrs. Nettel proclaimed. "He always makes our coffee. . . ." She eyed the steaming carafe on the counter with a firm nod.

"I'll pour whenever you're ready," Joy called after the sturdy figure sailing down the hallway.

When Mrs. Nettel finally did sit down at the table, it was to polish the silver punch bowl. Joy was standing at the window with her mug, staring out at the empty backyard.

"Missing the children, Sister?"

Joy slanted her a wistful look. "How perceptive of you, Mrs. N."

"Sometimes we don't know what we value until it's snatched away from us," she stated on a sigh, dipping her small rag into the jar of blue polish. "The irony of life."

So true. Watching Mrs. Nettel march through the house with a covetous air had drawn out a streak of envy in Joy. Her nesting instincts had gone haywire! And she should have seen it coming. She was growing roots here like she'd never known before. Dan was more than the heroic protector she'd dreamed of all those months on the run; he was her Mr. Right.

Though she'd cared for a man or two along the way, she'd never felt compelled to take care of one. And Dan accused her of setting the traps! Why, commitment was the biggest trap of all. One she'd fallen into here without a single sexual encounter.

But could Dan accept a partnership with a woman who wished to share his domain equally? He seemed so reluctant to share even his basic feelings and was alarmingly set in his ways. But he was capable of changing. True, the part in his hair wasn't much of a start....

"The children miss you, too," Mrs. Nettel was prattling on as she buffed. "You entertained them in such a professional way. The parents were so impressed." When Joy's mouth fell open over the term "professional," Mrs. Nettel promptly misread her apprehension. "Don't go modest on me now. It's a gift to have such a flair with children. I know what I'm talking about. Spent many years in the entertainment business, myself."

Joy's chest tightened. Enough mooning over romance. This was just the sort of information she'd hoped to collect. She fetched Mrs. Nettel a mug of coffee and joined her at the table. She strained to keep her voice within the tranquil boundaries she'd chosen for Sister Constance. "What did you do for a living?"

"Bookkeeper. But that's all behind me now," she added in swift dismissal. She polished harder, openly uncomfortable with the subject. Because of her link to Theo Nelson?

Joy shoveled three teaspoons of sugar into her coffee. Sweetened caffeine was the ultimate brain food. Her eyes shifted slightly behind her lenses as she sorted out the facts. Mrs. Nettel's visits to the Laff Trak were no doubt professional calls for bookkeeping. But that didn't necessarily make her part of the laundering racket. She could be completely honest. And she was long gone when the murder came to pass.

"I assume you're retired," Joy ventured.

Mrs. Nettel seemed startled by her curiosity. "Had my own business for twenty-five years." She released a humph from her large bosom. "Dan is like a son to me. Taking care of him is my biggest job now. I don't dwell on the past."

Even if there was an envelope jammed with money out there somewhere for Theo's false alibi? Even if a cop and a comic put away her former employer?

"Dan Burke seems like a wonderful person to have in one's life."

"The best!"

Joy wanted to believe in Mrs. Nettel. She seemed to deserve the fierce loyalty Dan had bestowed upon her. But loyalties could become as twisted as caramel taffy when pulled in enough directions. And surely it was no mere coincidence that someone so close to Theo had moved in next door to Dan after the Berkley trial.

But darn it all, Joy liked her a lot! There had to be a reasonable explanation for the setup. The temptation to confront her was strong. But Dan would hit the ceiling.

"I don't know how we got so far off the subject of you, Sister," Mrs. Nettel remarked. "But I was going to ask you about your goals, your vows."

Joy flushed, her hand shaking on her mug handle. "Why?"

"I have a producer friend at one of the local TV stations here in the Cities," she explained with a gleam of excitement. "He's looking for someone bright to host a new children's program he's developing. But I imagine with your duties, your old-fashioned order, you'd be unavailable for such a position."

Joy heart leaped to her throat. It was the perfect job. For Joy Jones. A new challenge for her creative muse. And daytime hours, the sort most people kept. Her hopes soon deflated, however. She couldn't go for the position without revealing her identity. "Unfortunately my duties are too erratic," she said with effort. "I could be called away at any time."

Mrs. Nettel clucked her tongue. "Such a pity. You fit so well into the neighborhood. And you've helped draw Dan out of his shell. The people around here are so delighted to finally have a word with him, to share the Christmas cheer. I've assured them all along that he's not the Scrooge he seems. But it is your presence that ultimately sold them."

"Well, my holiday work isn't a complete success," Joy protested, taking a sip of coffee. "Not with that prissy Christmas tree coming from the store!"

"I agree!" Mrs. Nettel trumpeted. "Half the fun of tree trimming is picking one out at a cold, windy stand in some parking lot. They're never perfect. Sort of tippy, with uneven branches. It's nature's way, for certain."

Joy's eyes rose toward heaven. "Blessedly true."

"At some point in history, the Burkes did some tree trimming themselves," Mrs. Nettel reported. "I found some lovely ornaments upstairs in the attic last summer. Antique-looking. Some of them hand carved."

"We could do it, you know," Joy proposed, her excitement rising.

Mrs. Nettel met her gaze with a twinkle. "I'll just dig out the department-store lady's name from his business-card file and have a word."

"Splendid!" Joy squeezed her eyes shut in ecstasy. Dan would be so pleased with the results that he would forgive her trip out with Mrs. Nettel. This neighbor just couldn't be against Dan. Not a woman who was willing to ferret through a drafty old attic for dusty ornaments and race around town searching for a spindly pine—all to stir up some Christmas magic.

As Joy and Mrs. Nettel piled into her station wagon for their errands, Dan was busy at his desk down at Metro Station. He was dividing his time between his reports and Joy's case, hoping to do justice to both. Often police work was a matter of going through the motions of tedious probing, hoping that something would click, somewhere, somehow. Time was running out. Joy couldn't hide at his place forever under the guise of Sister Constance Clarence.

Dan was more determined than ever to dig deep for answers, no matter how tough on his personal ties. His first resolution of the day had been to visit Records and request a check on Mrs. Nettel. Nearly everyone at the station knew of her smothering ways and teased him mercilessly on the subject. The young clerk had lifted her brows in speculation when Dan had removed his steam iron from a box, the household appliance covered with her prints. But she'd jumped into action just the same.

The next move was to contact Joy's landlord in Orlando. Dan hated giving away Faye/Joy's location, but he couldn't demand answers without identifying himself. He was going to trust Henry Sheldon's discretion solely on Joy's faith. She believed the old man could not be compromised, and she should know. Dan reached for the telephone, set it on top of a short stack of files and punched in the number for the Tropical Arms Apartments.

"Hello, Mr. Sheldon? This is Detective Dan Burke of the St. Paul Police Department. I'm the man investigating Faye Fairway's stalking allegations. Yes, she's still safe and sound.... I was wondering, sir, has there been any trouble on your end? Anyone lurking around... Quiet as usual, eh? No, she isn't with me now. I'll give her your best, of course. If anything develops, please call me.... No, at home would be best. I'll give you the number."

Dan grimaced in disappointment as he hung up. When was something going to shake loose? Just as he was about to set the phone back on the far corner of the desk, it rang in his hands.

"Detective Burke."

"Rex Cameron, please." The voice was male, clipped, and totally unfamiliar.

"I'm sorry, but he isn't in the office today."

"He's not at home, either.... Just called your department on a hunch."

"Rex does sometimes turn up on Saturdays." He grabbed a message pad and pencil. "Can I pass along your name?"

"Yes. Please tell him that his man at Thacker called to confirm the termination of our services as of yesterday."

"And the number where he can reach you?" The sharp point of the pencil broke off as Dan pressed it hard to the paper. The area code was the one he'd just called. Rex's man at Thacker—whatever that was—was out of Florida, as well.

"Got it?"

Dan gritted his teeth, keeping his voice even. "Yes. Thank you."

Dan slammed down the receiver in disappointment and suspicion. So what was Rex's connection in that part of the country? He hated like hell to pry. But somebody had taken Joy's Christmas card out of his private study. And what about that damn Rolex of his . . . ? With a deep breath he punched in the number on the pad.

"Thacker Corporation. How may I help you?"

Dan nodded in satisfaction. A different voice. Female. Probably a receptionist accustomed to answering questions every hour of the day. "I am thinking about engaging your services."

"Certainly, sir."

"Do you have an hourly price you can quote me?"

"Not really. It depends on the job. We generally set up a meeting for you with an operative. Your circumstance is reviewed and arrangements are made then."

If this wasn't a detective agency, he'd wear Joy's red wig to his own party tomorrow! "Thacker does investigative work, correct?"

"Correct."

"I'll get back to you once I check my calendar. Thank you very much."

Dan was frozen in time and space for a long time, his thumb pressed on the disconnect button, the receiver clamped to his ear. He loved Rex like a brother, but he had to consider the unthinkable. If Rex had gone after Joy, what would the reason be? Tying in the Rolex made Dan wonder if Rex was acting for someone else. Doing the legwork for someone else for pay. William Harris had money. Gwen had money, too. Theo Nelson might have money, too—the supposedly missing cash.

If Rex was in a financial bind—especially one that would cause him to betray his principles—all he had to do was ask him.

It was ten o'clock before Dan climbed the stairs to his bedroom that night. Joy was curled up in the window seat with an afghan, a paperback in front of her nose. Judging from the cover, it was not from his bookshelf. Certainly not Mrs. Nettel's conservative taste, either, with its bare-chested pirate embracing a blonde almost as beautiful as Joy herself. So where did it come from?

"Finally, copper," she blurted out in relief and complaint, stuffing one of his leather-tasseled bookmarks between the pages as though it were a scrap of paper.

"Sorry I'm late. There was a robbery on the north side and I had to investigate."

"See the tree?" she asked anxiously.

Dan regarded her with a frown. "No. Came straight up to check on you. Everything go all right with Mrs. Nettel?"

"Yeah, sure."

Joy shifted on the corduroy cushion. The afghan opened and he noted that she was dressed in yet another of his grungy sweatshirts. Their appeal was a mystery to him. "I tried to reach you a couple of times today."

Joy's nose wrinkled. "Guess I forgot all about the answering machine. Sorry."

"I let it ride until tonight, when I got disturbing news about Mrs. Nettel."

"Oh . . ." Her voice trailed off worriedly.

"When you didn't answer, I called her place, just to check her mood. She seemed quite jovial and normal, but I raced home as fast as I could, anyway."

Her delicate face grew grave. "Who is she, Danny?"

"I don't know yet. But she has no history before buying the house next door. She's covered her tracks well." Dan sighed hard, loosening his tie and collar.

She bit her lip. "So she's the one?"

He paced the floor in aggravation. "I don't know. At the very least she's a fraud. But Rex's position doesn't look too good, either. He's recently had some investigative work done in Florida." He touched her hair as she gasped in fear. "Your stalker could've been a private eye. Could've been hanging around to question you or confirm your identity. I just don't get it. If only we had a motive."

"Guess I'd better tell you what I know," she said with guilty resignation.

He pivoted toward the window seat, his face thunderous. "Tell me what?"

"That I've seen Mrs. Nettel at Theo's club a few times."

His roar counterpointed her squeaky confession.

"Don't get all huffy." She gave his hand a squeeze. "I held back for your own good."

"Your zany logic will be the death of me yet, lady," he swore softly.

"Well, I didn't want to hurt you needlessly. And I feel that Theo is sort of my territory—a black sheep I should check out."

"You aren't supposed to be checking out anybody!"

"Well, I spent the day with Mrs. Nettel and I am impressed with her sincerity," she countered defensively. "That's helpful, isn't it?"

"Tell me something I don't know about her, Joy," he challenged. "Did she happen to drop her reason for infiltrating my life? For changing her name?"

"Gee, no," she scoffed impatiently.

"You had no business keeping this from me."

"I was only trying to spare you," she maintained defiantly. "Until this name thing came up, I was certain she was innocent of any wrongdoing. That she was just an honest bookkeeper at the club."

Dan seized her shoulders. "Bookkeeper?"

"Something I deduced when I really wasn't checking out anybody," she replied smugly.

"Come on, honey, give!"

"Some gratitude!" she huffed with a toss of her head. "She said she'd been a bookkeeper for twenty-five years. Had her own business. Considers you a son."

"Actually, you're guessing about the Laff Trak job," he mused.

"It's deduction," she corrected proudly. "She met with Theo in his office. Not onstage, not in a booth. Just during the day in his office. Carried a briefcase sometimes."

"Good work," he conceded distractedly, rubbing his mouth.

Joy watched him sink lower and lower into himself. "I hate it when you get all moody, Dan, when you lock yourself away."

"I was just thinking that if Mrs. Nettel wanted to harm me, she could have done so a thousand times this past year."

Joy gulped. He'd been trying to spare her the alternative. "So she could've been hanging around you in the hopes of catching up with me," she speculated for him.

"We did discuss the possibilities. Revenge for Theo Nelson. The missing envelope of money."

"It just can't be her, Danny. She even offered me—the Sister—a job opportunity at a local television station. A show for kids."

Dan threw up his hands in despair. "She came over here to clean the house! How on earth did everything snowball so?"

"Things always snowball around me."

"She may have been testing you, hoping that you'd give yourself away."

Joy gulped. She'd almost done it, too. Aloud she said, "No. I still say my disguise is foolproof and she doesn't for a second believe I'm Joy Jones."

"You know I think it's good. We're betting your life on it." When her eyes grew wide with worry, he gave her bare knee a pat. "I'm not leaving you alone again until this is finished. We'll have to really keep our eyes open every minute, this weekend. People will be moving in and out of the house. Party guests, the servers."

"They'll all be here," she fretted.

He shook a heavy head. "I can't seem to scramble fast enough. Everything is so rushed, so intense."

"You may as well give it up for tonight," she consoled, uncurling from the window seat to wrap her arms around him. "Come down and see the tree."

The lines around his eyes deepened in weariness. "I'm ready to fall into bed, honey. A hot shower and the sheets are all I want."

"Please, Danny, just for me."

"I know what I paid for," he insisted flatly. "Every bough in place."

Joy tossed back her head with a huff of impatience. "You said you wanted me to have the best Christmas, and now you won't give me a minute of your time."

Dan rubbed his stiff, corded neck. "All right, you win. But only for a minute."

"Oh, good!" With holiday spirits promptly revived, she took him in tow.

"Freeze, copper!" she bit out the minute they entered the dark living room. "I've always wanted to say that," she confessed with a giggle, hurrying over to flick on the wall switch. Like magic the tree in the corner beside the grand piano lit up in a splash of color. "Super, huh?"

Dan stumbled forth, scanning the short crooked pine in sheer disbelief. "This isn't—You didn't—" He slowly turned on his heel to face her. "Where is my made-to-order tree?" he demanded. "My perfect, paid-for blue spruce. Guaranteed to tower exactly eight feet high up to my twelve-foot ceiling."

"Well, it's presently in a women's shelter," Joy reported with a cringe.

"I am a very generous man, Joy," he declared angrily. "I give plenty to the needy all year-round. I deserve the tree of my choice."

"You just don't get it, Danny," she said on a pleading note. "This tree isn't meant to be a sacrifice. Just the opposite." She linked her arm in his and drew him closer. "Come take a look."

Dan reached out to one of the arthritic branches, his huge hand closing around a homemade ornament, a plaster cut-out bell painted in green and gold, looped with a strand of red yarn. He closed his eyes, squared his shoulders, and looked as though he was about to explode. Exactly what emotion was fueling him, causing his body to quake like a churning volcano, was not yet clear.

"Mrs. Nettel and I got to talking," Joy babbled on nervously, wringing her hands. "She wanted to make things homey for you, too. She remembered the ornaments in the attic. . . ."

Joy paused, waiting for him to say something, anything. "I really don't think you understand, Dan. We put our heads together, ran our tails off to do this!" She circled his stiff form, her annoyance mounting. "Okay, so I wasn't supposed to leave the house. I was just fine as the nun. If it's the paperback that's bothering you, Mrs. Nettel didn't see me buy it. I went into a bookstore alone. The clerk didn't bat an eye over the pirate on the cover. I'm sure she figured it was a present for some friend—"

"Enough, Joy! It's not the book, it's not the AWOL."

"But you are furious," she pressed. "Not touched, not grateful, just downright livid!"

"You assumed way, way too much here," he growled, releasing the molded bell as though it were suddenly aflame in his palm. "You went way too far. I don't want to recapture ghostly childhood Christmases, wallow in gooey holiday sentimentality. I keep a deliberate distance from such things. Joy, I sympathize with your needs. I thought if I tried, I could fulfill some of them." He gave his head a rueful shake. "I naively hoped you'd accept my celebration as it was. But no, you barged in and upset the status quo, tried to change all the things I count on!"

"I was only trying to make it better," she tearfully explained.

"Not better. Not for me."

"Tell me exactly what I've done!" she cried out in bewilderment.

He hurled her a dark, silent look.

"Talk to me, Danny, please."

"I can't." His body radiated with pain. With hands clenched to his sides he strode stiffly out of the room and up the squeaky stairs.

Joy waited in the stillness during those next crucial minutes, hoping that he'd think better of his exit. But the old pipes creaked in the walls as water surged up through them to the floor above. He was taking the shower he so badly wanted.

She began to prowl the room. The feeble little tree laden with a hodgepodge of ornaments was nothing more than a symbol of herself. Mismatched. Out of balance.

How could she ever have hoped to permanently crash through his reserve? Wheedle him into a merging of body and soul? She'd bared all her secrets to him, trusted him with her life, and he wouldn't explain about one crummy tree!

With an angry lunge, she grabbed two of the pine's prickly branches and tipped over the whole works. It

bounced to the carpet with a rustle, needles and ornaments flying. As she would fly! She marched on to the
foyer with purpose, the soles of Gwen's old fuzzy red
slippers slapping on the tiles, the waistband of the
Notre Dame sweatshirt rising on her hip with every
stride. With no thought to her lounging attire, she
grabbed Dan's chilly woolen topcoat from the parson's bench, pulled it over her shoulders and hurled out
the front door.

The wild blonde in the ankle-length coat and fuzzy
secondhand slippers probably would have interested
any neighbor who was awake and watching. But the
avenue was deserted with the approach of midnight,
save for the twinkling strings of colored lights adorn-
ing the rooflines and windowsills. Mrs. Nettel had
mentioned that everyone had their lights on a timer, to
be a merry welcome to any stray resident arriving home
late. Now the adornments seemed garish and insincere
to Joy. Just a bunch of bulbs with no spirit behind them.

Joy paused on the sidewalk, fresh tears chilling her
cheeks.

All undressed and nowhere to go.

8

Jack Frost nipping . . .

DAN STOOD IN THE CENTER of the tub, the tepid jet spray pounding his taut, muscular body. A huge naked warrior, strong and powerful and unshakable. A threat to the bad guys. A bigger threat to himself. He lathered the soap on his biceps, his shoulders, sloshing and spewing his way to his face. It would take forever for hot water to tunnel through the pipes, but it was just as well. He deserved to be punished with a jolting slap from something. Or someone.

He'd been bound and determined to keep Joy away from the last remaining tender button inside him. But she was just too good.

And he was just plain stupid. How could he have hoped to fulfill her visions, without suffering from the fallout of his own bleak Christmases past? The scars of his lonely childhood had faded considerably because of his careful treading, year after year, through the emotional land mines of the season.

He knew now that it was time to let go of them completely. Start fresh with a new foundation.

Joy, the little firecracker, had seen it first—recognized that at thirty he was in a now-or-never position. He had to break loose from his rut. This shock tonight held just enough wattage to jolt him to life. All he wanted now was the chance to start over with Joy; learn to celebrate Christmas present in a whole new way. . . .

He would learn to accept change. In the neighborhood. In his own house. In his own heart.

He would explain his horrid behavior. Right now.

The slam of the front door below jarred him as he stepped out of the tub. What was happening?

Dan toweled down with lightning speed, then threw on his terry robe as he charged down to the foyer, all the while telling himself that Joy would never leave the house. But his topcoat was gone.

Maybe she was still in the yard. He pulled open the front door for a peek. She'd left the gate gaping open. He swiveled on his bare heels in search of footwear. His galoshes were on a mat under the parson's bench. He shoved them on, and for the first time in his life, didn't stop to lace them. Cinching the sash of his robe tightly at his waist, Dan barreled down the steps.

He paused at the gate. She was standing on the street corner, four houses away. "Joy!" he called out through megaphoned hands. "Come home."

She jumped at the sound of his voice, a frightened blonde huddled under the glow of the streetlamp. "Go away."

Dan's boots clomped along the shoveled concrete in pursuit, the cool night air whirling up inside his robe like an ice maiden's sigh. It was damn lucky the temperature was above freezing, he thought, with that foolish girl running around in almost nothing at all!

Joy crossed the street to the park the moment he began to move, the hem of the huge topcoat swirling around the toes of her fluffy red slippers.

"Not the park, Joy!" Dan muttered in low-voiced helplessness.

The Pendham Park Reserve was a lovely place during the day, a nature wonderland designed for recreation and relaxation. A network of blacktop paths made the entire area accessible on foot or bike, with all trails leading to the small lake in the center. In the summertime, kids frolicked under the trees, joggers pounded the paths, and teens necked on the benches, all to the tune of quartets playing atop the grassy knolls. During the winter, however, traffic on the grounds slowed considerably. Joggers, walkers and skaters visited in smaller numbers, generally in the daylight.

Dan crossed the street, pausing at the brick-arch entrance. In the park without his pants? His life was a shambles!

"Joy!" he called out again desperately. "Please come back!" Dan melded into the hollow of the arch as a car passed by, searching the immediate area for a sign of life. When nothing stirred, he turned up the collar of his robe and forged ahead.

The grounds were utterly and fortunately deserted. The only sound on the trail was the crunch of the snow beneath Dan's boots, the occasional snap of a twig. He tried one route, then another, keeping a keen ear trained for any sound of life. Finally, he heard a soft whimpering cry in the stark night air. "Joy! Honey!"

"You are a total loss, copper! I thought I was a mess—" She jabbed a finger at him, standing there in his robe and galoshes. "But you—you, mister, are a disaster. Always pulling back. Always in control."

"Do I look like a man in control?" he hollered, glaring down at his hairy bare legs.

She hung her head in mourning, hugging herself for warmth. "Nothing can make you crack. If Joy Jones can't rattle your cage, you're a hopeless case."

Dan captured her face in his hands and drew it inches from his own. "Don't underestimate yourself. You've finally done it. Stripped me inside out!"

Joy squirmed as his dark eyes drilled into her.

"You ferreted out my last secret," he accused roughly. "Those ornaments of mine and Gwen's, they're badges of pain, of loneliness and despair. They were buried in the attic on purpose."

Realization flooded her blotchy face. "Oh, no. You should've told me sooner, Dan. Confided in me when I confided in you."

"I—I didn't think it would be necessary, Joy."

"Not necessary to open up your heart to me? And don't tell me you've never done it. That's no excuse. Not when I love you so."

Dan's hands moved down the slope of her shoulders, buried inside his enormous topcoat. "You love me?"

"Yes, you stupid man, I do!"

"Well, in all your chattering, you never said so."

"I was afraid," she confessed, dropping her gaze. "Afraid you wouldn't love me back."

"Well, I do love you," he assured quietly. "Enough to tell you the truth if you want to hear it." When she tilted her gaze back up in anticipation, he forced himself to begin. "Gwen and I were a couple of very lonely kids. My father took full advantage of his senatorial connections, as did my mother. Their idea of holiday celebration was dining around town with cronies. They found hearth and home a boring alternative to political functions. We were given only the most perfunctory attention, then left to the household staff. It bonded Gwen and me together in a tight relationship that no one else has fully understood." His mouth curved slightly with a pensive pause. "Although 'controlling,' 'overbearing' and 'protective' are descriptions that fit both of us to a T."

"But why on earth do you continue on with the holiday reception year after year?" she demanded.

"Because it's the one tradition that we looked forward to as children," he sought to explain. "It was the one time at Christmas when our parents were home. When they wanted us to shine, to join in on the fun. Not very sensible, is it?"

"No!" she cried in approval. "Nothing sensible about it at all! Downright crazy, really."

With a darting look up and down the snow-dusted trail, Dan seized Joy by the arms and drew her into a cluster of trees. "You want crazy? I'll show you crazy!" He plowed on through the brush, crowding her up against a huge oak tree well off the beaten path. This physical reunion had been a long time coming. And it wouldn't keep another second. Leaning into her trembling body, he stroked the tender length of her throat, his thumb pressing into her jumping pulse point. He quaked in his boots as she responded to his touch with an earthy, needy moan.

"I want you so much, Danny. Deep, deep, inside me."

Joy was so open, so responsive, so willing to express her needs. And so beautiful in the sliver of moonlight angling down between the bare branches overhead. Her yellow hair spilled everywhere like liquid honey. Her eyes sparkled like twin pools of seawater. He couldn't resist her any longer. Making love to her had been the sweetest thing in his life. *Damn the control, damn the danger, damn the whole damn world!*

His fingers flipped open the only two buttons she'd bothered to fasten. The coat fell open around her small body, huddled beneath his shaggy college sweatshirt. He began to caress her, first over the shirt, then beneath it, bunching the fleece fabric up over her bare hips, then higher and higher up to her chest. She gasped in wonder as he dipped down to cup the fleshy undersides of her breasts and guide them to his mouth. He lavished her nipples with hot, wet sucks, then withdrew to let the cold air harden them to icy pebbles.

"How's this for lunacy?" he rasped hungrily against her ear.

"Delicious."

A sweep of cold air between his legs told him that she'd undone the sash of his robe. Her fingers skated in the nest of hair below his navel, flicking, exploring, teasing his shaft to life.

"Time sure isn't a luxury out here," he growled ruefully. In response, Joy snaked her arms up around his neck, drawing him down. Skin singed skin in the cold darkness. Dan wanted to throw himself into her fire and fry to a cinder.

"I want to feel you, honey," he hissed in harsh longing.

"Then hurry up and climb inside, copper," she invited through chattering teeth.

Dan joined her in the coat, lifting her clear off the ground as his hands slid under her armpits. He turned a half circle until he was the one against the tree. Bracing himself against the trunk he lowered her to his hipbone and over his erection. She was feather light, an elfinlike temptress poised over him with the ultimate fruit. With a catlike look she pulled the topcoat's woolen lapels over his shoulders, cloaking their union behind its silky-soft lining.

She rested her forearms on his shoulders, digging her soft inner thighs into his waist. "How . . ."

"Just keep us covered. I'll do the rest."

Clasping her bottom he guided her over his shaft. With a lusty groan into the silent velvet night, she swallowed him up inside her.

Pressure churned from his core as Dan sliced into Joy's folds of femininity. He shut his eyes, his focus a piercing red point against the back of his lids. He'd been a human volcano for days, on the verge of eruption. Now the fire surged through his body with blinding force, reaching every inch of him. Escalating swiftly toward explosion.

Within seconds, climax overcame them both. Dan lolled against the unforgiving bark of the tree, his broad chest heaving. Joy was a limp doll in his arms, showering his face with small kisses. They sank unthinkingly into a blanket of snow below. Impact with the cold ground, however, snapped them back to their senses—and to their feet.

"Let's get the hell home," Dan muttered, drawing her close.

Joy touched his arm. "I have to warn you, Danny, I think I wrecked my poor little Christmas tree."

"How?"

Joy bit her lip in distress. "I sort of tipped it over."

"Don't worry," he soothed, buttoning her snugly back into the coat. "I have a feeling it'll look much the same once we set it up again."

Relief crossed her face. "Really?"

Dan nodded. Just how much damage could she have caused the poor decrepit thing?

"C'mon," she piped up with a laugh. "I'll race ya."

Actually it was the wintry air they were pitted against, as it chased after them like a shrew with a rolling pin, right up to Dan's front steps.

"It can't be true!" Joy lamented as Dan leaned a shoulder against the front door of the Castle, giving the knob another fierce rattle.

"No mistake," Dan flatly confirmed. "We're locked out, all right."

"So what are we going to do now?"

"Go next door to Mrs. Nettel's."

Joy set her hands on her hips. "For what? Hot cocoa?"

"For the spare key," he reluctantly admitted.

"But you said she didn't have one!"

"I told you she didn't have one so you wouldn't insist on having one."

Joy stomped a fuzzy red slipper on the stoop. "Well, why couldn't I have one, Danny?"

"Because I was afraid you'd be tempted to break out."

"That's dumb!"

"Well, on a scale of dumb, standing out here ranks supreme."

Joy sighed. "You're right. But gee whiz, copper. What else haven't you told me?"

"I'm bare down to the soul," he vowed with a flap of his robe. Joy wasn't amused. "Look, I gave her the key for emergencies like this—well, something like this. You can understand. She's my housekeeper. She's seen everything in my place—right down to the ornaments in my attic. I didn't want to ask for it back after you showed up. It would only have aroused her natural curiosity. And I did put those security bolts on the inside, didn't I? To keep her or anyone else from just waltzing in with a key."

"Your trust is doled out to such a chosen few," Joy accused unhappily, "but boy, when you give it out, you're like a naive kid loaning his bike to a stranger."

Dan's dark eyes widened with emotion. "You oughtta know, stranger."

Joy reared back with a gasp. "Well, I brought the bike back, didn't I?"

Dan grinned in pure pleasure. "Yeah. Thanks for the joyride."

Joy pointed toward Mrs. Nettel's house with a sputter. "You—you just get over there, mister, and get that key!"

"I will." With the crook of a finger he said, "First come 'round to the back."

Joy's eyes slitted in suspicion. "Why, copper?"

"Because, my sugar-coated baby, we have to switch candy wrappers."

Joy gawked in horror. "What!"

"C'mon, c'mon," he prodded, grabbing her by the elbow. "The temperature's dropping and I'd hate to find out what freezes off below thirty degrees."

Mrs. Nettel didn't answer the bell right away. Dan shifted from one foot to the other on her front porch, trying to peer through the square window beside the door. He felt like he was in a Christmas window dis-

play amid the twinkling lights strung in generous supply across the entire face of the house. Didn't these
holiday maniacs ever shut the things off?

"Try her knocker," Joy hissed, peeking out from the
bushes near the house, her hand clenched to the collar
of Dan's robe at her throat.

"What a tarty thing to say!" Dan retorted under his
breath.

"You know what I mean—*her silver door knocker.*"

She had a right to be testy, he inwardly acknowledged. The robe was a whole lot colder than the topcoat. But a trade had been necessary. He and Mrs.
Nettel weren't on those sorts of terms!

There was movement on the other side of the door a
moment later. Mrs. Nettel's roller-encrusted head
peered out the window at him.

"My stars, Dan!" She whisked open the door, her
pale eyes wide in disbelief. "Are you in trouble? Is there
a prowler?"

He shook his tousled black head. "I don't want to
come in, Mrs. Nettel," he declined politely as she
tugged at his coat sleeve. "Unfortunately I've locked
myself out and need the key you keep for me."

Her hands flew to her cheeks. "Lands, I'm not sure
where it is!"

Joy's gasp of indignation cut the stillness.

Mrs. Nettel stepped out onto the porch, her flowing
flannel nightie billowing at her ankles.

"There's a blonde in my bushes," she noted with a
humph.

Joy poked her head out, then back in like a turtle.

"I see her distinctly, Detective." She turned back to
Dan, shivering beside her with his hands in his pock-

ets. For the first time she took full stock of his appearance—from his unlaced boots to his bare calves, to his buttoned-up topcoat.

Dan fidgeted under the inspection, as a randy eighteen-year-old might. "I'm sorry, Mrs. N. I wouldn't have drawn you into these personal circumstances unless it was an emergency."

She tipped her rollered head toward him in consultation. "I'm a woman of the world, myself, dear. But what of our beloved Sister Constance Clarence? Surely you wouldn't allow her to witness such high jinks."

"No, no," he assured her with a wave. "She's away. Won't be back until tomorrow."

She gave him a pleased nod. "Ah. Well, I hope you discreetly usher this one out before she returns," she said quietly. "Wouldn't want to upset Sister. She is the cat's."

The cat's. Mrs. Nettel's ultimate compliment. Joy could charm anybody—*as* anybody!

"Give me a minute and I'll hunt up that key," she promised abruptly. "Put it in a cupboard in the kitchen...."

"Hang on," he placated to the rustling bushes. "She'll be right back."

"She doesn't even appreciate the key!" Joy fumed from her hiding spot. "If it were mine, I'd know exactly where it is. I'd have a separate key ring with my initials engraved on a gold disk. I'd cherish it forever and ever! I'd—"

"Shut up! You're going to get a key of your own!"

The door swung open in the wake of his words. "Here it is, Dan," she announced, pressing it into his palm.

Dan bowed slightly. "Thank you very much!"

"Wouldn't give the blonde a key," she advised under her breath. "What you need is a girl like the Sister. One who isn't a nun, of course," she added hastily. "Good night, out there!" she called awkwardly before slamming the door shut.

"'Wouldn't give the blonde a key,'" Joy grumbled later on between the toasty sheets of Dan's bed. "The cheek. Marry a girl like the Sister. The cheek."

"Give her a break. She barely got a look at you out in the bushes."

Joy splayed herself across his chest, toying with the coarse hairs circling his nipples. "I suppose she'll grow to like me just as I really am. If she isn't the stalker."

"Sure, she will. Besides, you've got the Pendham Avenue market cornered on cheek," he growled, stroking the smooth curve of her bottom beneath the covers.

Joy purred under his caress. They were in a supremely sated state, having just returned from a carnal journey of rediscovery in Dan's warm king-size bed. They were just dozing off when Joy thought of Mrs. Nettel's advice. Alert again, Joy couldn't resist garnering some reassurances.

"Danny, you think you made a mistake, letting go and loving me?"

"I feel totally incapable of another lucid thought," he confided in bewilderment.

She nipped at his neck. "Be serious!"

"I am." He raised himself up on his pillow, tucking Joy in the hollow of his shoulder.

"Nothing's really changed," she protested. "You just acted on your feelings. You're still your steady old self."

He arched a heavy black brow. "Oh, yeah? My emotions are all swimming just beneath the surface in a vat of nitroglycerin. One spill could rocket me into oblivion."

"Oops, better not jiggle you too much anymore tonight."

"Let's not jiggle at all again until tomorrow," he advised, giving her shoulders a light squeeze. "I'm totally beat."

She frowned. "I hope I can doze off, with the party on my mind. . . ."

Dan sighed with a trace of impatience. "We settled this. You'll be safe as the nun."

Joy sat up to meet his face squarely. "That's what I've been thinking about."

Dan groaned. "I wish you wouldn't."

"Maybe I've been playing it too safe."

"Can't play it too safe."

Joy fluttered her lashes. "Tell that to my fool-for-love in the park!"

"This fool ultimately had the good sense to come back in from the cold. And intends to get some sorely needed sleep." With a punch to his pillow, Dan eased back under the sheets. "Forget any harebrained ideas about putting yourself in jeopardy."

"About the tree . . ."

"Righting it back in its stand was good enough for tonight. Just as I predicted, it looks as good as ever."

"Guess I can straighten out the ornaments first thing in the morning."

"To your little heart's content."

With a sultry sound Joy snuggled against his length. "It's okay to do this from now on, isn't it, Danny? I can't tempt you unfairly anymore, can I?"

"It's very okay, honey," he rumbled in pleasure as she melded against his spine. "Though I have the notion that you'll be nothing but unfair temptation for as long as we both shall live."

9

Later on we'll conspire . . .

FACING PRISON INMATE Theo Nelson was not going to be easy. But there was no turning back now. This was the last place she wanted to be on a Sunday morning right before Christmas. Joy gulped back her apprehension as she eased into a chair opposite him.

A mere table between them—she hadn't been this close since his arrest.

She stared into his fleshy oval face, with its flinty piercing eyes and thick curled lips. Before the lid was ripped off his dirty dealings, she had viewed Theo as a Dutch uncle, a moody but amusing pal. Had she acted too impulsively this time, coming here under Dan's strident objections? Joy was viewing her old boss objectively for the first time ever. Dan had insisted upon that agonizing exercise this morning over breakfast when she'd proposed the visit.

The facts were clear now, a year later. Theo had been a hard case all along. He wasn't the gruff, misunderstood bear who was really true blue beneath it all. He was a crook who'd coerced her into a perilous high-speed chase with the police. Who had risked her life with no qualms whatsoever. She smiled at him in tentative greeting.

"So, how have you been, Theo?"

Theo drew a humorless smirk as he scanned her face full of stage makeup and her lime-green polyester pantsuit. "If it ain't Esther Emerson, the busybody neighbor who doesn't gossip, only listens."

"Right out of my old trunk of tricks," Joy quipped with a lopsided grin.

"Thought maybe the name was a fluke, that there was some do-gooder waiting out here for me."

"I am a do-gooder, Theo."

"Not by me you ain't," he denied. "Not after the stunt you pulled. You may as well have delivered me here in a tied-up package."

Yeah, right. A three-hundred-pound package of blubber and gristle. Joy had felt guilty about turning him in for too darn long. Facing him now, with the feelings of family, of friendship, forever squashed, she saw him realistically for what he really was: a common user. The nerve of him and Jerome Berkley claiming that they were together during her show! When all the while Berkley was home killing his wife... And now Theo had the gall to blame her for his situation! She clenched her fists under the table. But the smile barely wavered. She was here with purpose: to jumpstart the stalker.

That was how she'd put it to Dan. Only a few short days had passed since she'd landed back in the Twin Cities, taking refuge in his home. While it was a relief to be hidden away, it had pushed her stalker back into the shadows. Dan had clues, suspects, but nothing concrete. A trap was the only answer. Force the stalker out in the open by revealing that she was back in town. Theo seemed like a logical place to start.

Dan had argued this move vehemently. He knew what losing Theo—or losing her untarnished image of him—meant to her. Dan had pointed out that Theo could probably still damage her emotionally; that the people closest to her were the most adept at it. Joy was understanding Dan's hard shell more and more every day. He'd learned to protect his tender inner self from those around him in a gradual process that had started in childhood.

"Nothin' but a squealer, Joy," Theo raged.

"Gee whiz, Theo, Lieutenant Berkley murdered his wife!"

He sighed impatiently. "Yeah, yeah. Destroyed our whole laundering operation, too. All because of a dame. Always is."

"Did you know what kind of alibi he was buying?" she demanded.

"No, I—" He cut himself off, then addressed her with a jab of a thick finger. "Listen, girl, Berkley bought nothing from me. No money passed between us. Berkley was the boss. I was the front man. I did what I was told."

"Yeah, yeah," Joy echoed in sullen imitation. She'd seen that money with her own eyes.

"The cops believed me," he insisted. "I acted out of fear."

Theo did have his phobias, Joy knew. Driving a car and tolerating heights were big ones.

Theo grunted under her dubious look. "So what are you doing here?"

"Just came for a friendly holiday visit."

His blunt face wavered as he weighed her words. "Never came before."

"I was on the run," she said matter-of-factly. "I made a couple of shady cops real nervous. They were gunning for me."

"Maybe I did hear about that," he admitted, running a hand through the small patch of brown hair on the center of his head. "So everything is okay now?"

"Somebody else is stalking me now," she informed him, careful not to accuse. "That's the reason for the disguise. I'm back in the Twin Cities, but hiding out."

"So you wonder if Uncle Theo here can pull some strings and find out what it's all about," he assumed smugly, tilting back in his chair.

The arrogant ass! He'd be the last person she'd rely on for anything. But let him think what he pleased. "Could you, Theo?" she asked sweetly. "You have so many connections."

"Why should I?" he snorted, knitting his fingers across his barrel chest. "You were a friend, somebody I expected to keep her mouth shut."

It took all her self-control not to lunge at him in fury. "And you, choir boy, took me hostage!"

"The gun wasn't even loaded," he snapped defensively. "And I was desperate to get away." He shrugged in self-absolution. "Say, you didn't tell anybody about how scared I was during the chase, did you?"

"You mean how you held the gun on me the whole way?" she challenged.

"Naw, how I held the statue of the saint the whole way," he muttered under his breath, shifting in obvious discomfort.

"I only mentioned it to Detective Burke," she replied honestly. "Who would care?" She grinned crookedly.

"Funny thing is, the Church has relieved St. Christopher of his travel title. Ironic, huh?"

"You should still treat that statue with respect," he scolded.

"Sure, Theo." Joy knew him to be superstitious as well as phobic.

"So that junker of yours still running?"

Joy folded her arms across her lime-green jacket. "Yes. And it's not a junker. It just couldn't outrun a rally of squad cars at a hundred miles an hour."

"Don't get riled. Just wondered how you got here."

"By taxi," she replied. "I'm back, but my car is not."

He squinted in confusion.

"I lent it to a friend," she explained huffily. "One who appreciates a favor. And a great piece of machinery." She pinched her lips together. She was preaching, after her inner vow not to.

"You're too trusting of people, Joy. Just like your old buddy Theo, here."

Theo and Joy, a pair of lovable patsies, out for a joyride in her poor clunker of a car! Joy had forgotten just how blind Theo was to his own shortcomings.

"I didn't mean you any harm," he insisted under her leery look.

"Maybe I'd better be going," she declared suddenly. Dan had been right. It was hard to face this part of her past. And she'd done her schtick, revealed her return. Waiting to see if he rose to the bait was the next phase.

"Don't go yet," he swiftly interceded as she rose to her feet. "I don't expect too many visitors this week, and it is Christmas...."

He was appealing to her sentimental side. She knew it, but she sat back down anyway.

"You been doing any stage work since my place closed?" he asked.

"No, I've just been surviving. Moving around and staying safe."

"You're a good comic," he conceded with a trace of reluctance. "You should be working."

"I will be," she assured him, with a lift to her chin. "And what are your plans? You must have some, with half your sentence served."

"I'm going to miss the club, I know that much," he grumbled. "You know when I started up ten years ago, I was straight all the way. Somehow, the crooked edges closed in."

Joy bit her lip. Theo would always see himself as a victim. "So start over, Theo," she suggested brightly.

"Maybe, maybe . . . Far away from here."

Would Mrs. Nettel be moving on with him? Joy desperately wanted to squeeze her into the conversation, but couldn't afford to alert Theo to the fact that she'd met Mrs. Nettel through Dan. It would pinpoint her current hideout in a hurry! If they were in cahoots, they'd easily figure out that she was Sister Constance Clarence. Yet it seemed like such a waste not to try, after coming this far.

"So, anybody from the club ever come to visit?" Joy asked conversationally.

"A couple of the waitresses, Gina and Jackie. And Barry from the bar."

"What about that older lady?" she probed, with an innocent flutter of lashes.

"Which one?"

Joy feigned uncertainty. "You know the one. . . . The one who got under your skin. The bookkeeper."

"Oh." He froze in reflection. "I told you about her?"

"Why sure, you must have. I know she was your bookkeeper, don't I?"

"Yeah, well, I don't want to talk about her." His glassy eyes narrowed keenly. "Skip it, okay?"

"Done and done, Theo. I can't even remember her name, after all...." She trailed off expectantly, but Theo wasn't rising to the bait. His meaty shoulders and chins were stubbornly hunched. No way was he going to reveal Mrs. Nettel's real name. Carefully disguising her disappointment, she moved on to lighter subjects.

"Well, thanks for coming," he begrudgingly said about twenty minutes later. "Can I call you, if I feel like it?"

Was it a trap? "Sorry, Theo, but I'm moving around like crazy," she lied smoothly. "Some nights I'm staying in St. Paul. Other nights in Minneapolis. I won't feel secure until this stalker is found."

"Yeah, sure. Wouldn't want to deliberately get you into any trouble."

Joy shook her head ruefully. "No, Theo, not you."

A cab emblazoned with Bayport's Best was waiting for her outside. She climbed into the back seat, closing out a gust of arctic air. The temperature had fallen fifteen degrees since her tryst with Dan last night in the park. Tonight, after the party, they'd skip the outdoor appetizer and move directly up to the bedroom.

"Where can I take you, ma'am?" the driver asked as he started the meter.

"Back to Bayport, to the diner where you picked me up, please," she requested, settling back in the seat.

The short trip seemed to be over as soon as it started. Joy tipped the driver generously and hustled into the small homey restaurant.

All the locals glanced up at her as she entered, a little old lady in the lime-green pantsuit topped with a man's bulky blue ski jacket. She circled around the bustling lunch counter, heading for the table in back where she'd had a cup of coffee earlier. An arm snaked out of a booth and into her path, giving her jacket a sharp tug.

"Oh, it's you!" she said, breathlessly tumbling onto the bench beside Dan.

"Of course, it's me. Don't tell me you managed to make new friends even in here."

"In this getup?" she squawked. "So why did you change tables?"

"Because this booth is more comfortable," Dan explained, leaning back on the red vinyl cushion. "The time's been dragging since you left."

Joy flashed him a grateful smile as she slipped off her jacket. Once she'd convinced Dan that she must see Theo, he had leaped into action. He spoke to the warden at Stillwater prison by telephone, clearing the Esther/Joy visit. He'd driven her to the adjoining town of Bayport, reluctantly but objectively deciding that he should remain out of sight, so no one could make his car and license plate at the prison. Though the warden was an old friend of his late father's who could be implicitly trusted, the prison walls had a thousand prying eyes that could not be.

Why was every reunion with Joy such an emotional upheaval? Dan was wondering. He caught his reflection in the side of the napkin dispenser on the table and discovered that he was beaming like a schoolboy. This was the sort of lover he'd always wanted to be. Flushed, rushed and uninhibited. Joy had a way of bringing out the very best in him. And who'd ever have thought Christmas could really be a whimsical time of year?

Dan turned his attention to Joy, who was rattling off an enormous food order to the waitress. He didn't even blink in disapproval when she ordered two kinds of pie for dessert.

"Double all of that, please," he chimed in jovially.

Joy's gray head spun in surprise. "I believe I may be a bad influence on you!"

"And so proud of it," he teased, stroking her chin. He paused as the waitress returned with water and Coke drinks, then encouraged her to report what had happened.

"The goof actually thought I wanted him to check out my stalker through his connections," she related in a hush.

Dan's features sharpened. "Think he meant it?"

"I don't know. He's still in a denial mode about the payoff from Berkley. And he's reasoned away why he forced me into that high-speed chase with him before his arrest. He thinks I let him down!"

"Did he ask you any questions?"

"Oh, he asked if my car was still on the road. Wondered if I'd told anyone how scared he'd been during the chase, clutching that statue and all. He seemed relieved to hear that only you know about it." Joy shook her head.

"The gun was the important thing," Dan commented. "But I suppose he doesn't want to look like a bigger coward than he already does."

"He also tried to find out where I was staying."

Dan rotated his water glass. "He say anything about Mrs. Nettel?"

Joy patted his arm. "Nothing incriminating. But I did trick him into admitting that she was the Laff Trak bookkeeper at some point. Said he didn't want to talk about her."

"Was he angry with her?"

"I don't know."

"So he may very well have been protecting her."

Joy nodded with a contrite smile. "Yes, Danny. I'm sorry."

"I'm sorry Theo turned out to be such a bastard, for your sake," Dan returned with a sad smile.

"Trusting the wrong people can happen to anyone," she consoled. "Me with Theo. You with Mrs. Nettel. When people meet our needs, it's tough not to be drawn in. If Theo had been straight—as I thought he was—he probably could've made me a local celebrity. I believed in his talents and his intentions."

"And we know all the maternal touches given me by Mrs. Nettel, turned me into a jellyfish."

"Naw, maybe a cuddly teddy bear looking for warm fuzzies."

Joy leaned over to press her mouth to his, gasping in surprise when Dan turned his cheek to her. "This is a public place, Esther," he admonished. "You've forgotten that you're thirty years my senior in that costume of yours."

"The hell I did, copper," she purred with a wink. "Just imagine the pleasure it would give the senior lady customers to see one of their own scoring big. C'mon, be a sport."

"No, Mother," he retorted loudly, before dropping his voice back down. "It would be ridiculous to call attention to us."

"Oh, all right," she said in a huff. Her features softened, however, when she felt his hand squeezing her thigh under the table. "You do care," she marveled in pleasure.

"I'm just plain crazy about you," he said.

"You know, someday I'm going to look a whole lot like Esther, here," she cautioned, taking a sip of her Coke.

Dan nodded in concession. "Nature's fate for all of us."

"It won't bother you, then?"

"Not at all, my darling," he assured, angling his arm along the cushion behind her. "Unless . . ."

"Unless what?" she demanded bleakly.

"Unless you insist on wearing that hideous green polyester pantsuit!"

"Well, I plan to hang on to it," she informed him with a lift to her chin. "You just might go through a middle-age crisis or something and come to demand this sort of gal. And you can't get this neon double-knit just any old place anymore."

Dan exhaled, raising his eyes to the ceiling. "I imagine landfills are brimming with it."

Joy ignored his gibe, twisting around toward the lunch counter. "Waitress!" she reedily chirped with a wave. "I meant to mention that I'd like my pie along with the entrée."

"Certainly, ma'am," she replied cheerily. "Would your son like his, as well?"

She pursed her lips and clucked in regret. "I think not, m'dear. His just desserts must come in the end."

"IT'S ALMOST PARTY TIME," Dan called out later that night as he exited the bathroom, cleanly shaven and comfortably naked. He rounded the bedroom doorway, stopping short at the sight of Joy standing at the dresser in her skimpy pink nylon panties and enormous bra stuffed plump with twin grapefruits.

"I know what you're thinking," she complained, setting a hand on her tiny waist. "Gee whiz, what a Christmas present it would be if those grapefruits were really part of the package."

"No, I wasn't." He pulled her up against his muscled body, gently wedging his knee into her pelvis. "Might be intriguing, just for one night...."

Joy's retort was lost in a gasp of pleasure as Dan urged her up over his knee. The satiny fabric of her panty scraping his hair-roughened skin caused an exquisite friction at her intimate opening. Grasping his waist in her hands she mounted his thigh, scaling its length with an undulating motion that inflamed her. Cupping her bottom in his hands he pushed her up and down his leg again and again with guttural groans of encouragement. On her plane of desire there was no party, no danger—nothing but an exquisite burn.

Joy opened her eyes as Dan inhaled with a shudder. His shaft was erect as he set her back on her bare feet, dropping to his knees before her.

"It's almost time for the party," she whispered in reluctant warning. "Mrs. Nettel and the servers will be here soon."

His reply against her belly was inaudible and inconsequential.

Joy raked her fingers through his thatch of raven hair as he planted tiny kisses around her navel. Impromptu lovemaking was the most exciting to her—rushed, impetuous and spontaneous.

All the things Dan ordinarily was not.

But he'd been a different man since last night in the park. Impulsive and insatiable. He obviously expected no objection to his seductive overtures. And why should he, considering this was their third tryst of the day?

She writhed with mounting passion as his tongue traveled along the elastic of her panties. With nimble shoplifter fingers he peeling them off her hipbone. The scrap of nylon shielding her secrets fell to a useless fluff of fabric at her feet.

With one last shred of rational thought, she acknowledged that the control he lived by was gone in a ball of consuming fire. He had so wanted to remain celibate, alert. Ever since their lovemaking in the park, he'd been taking gambles he'd have otherwise scoffed at. Intellectually, she knew she should feel some remorse, be concerned. But she was so delighted with his new persona, that she couldn't help luxuriating in it.

Joy's inner duel ended here. Dan's hands were at her inner thighs now. His tongue forged for entry into her intimate opening, a licking flame singeing her with wet heat. Joy stood over him, her fingers pressing into his shoulders, paralyzed by the mounting sensations within her. She soon cried out in abandonment as her passion reached its climax and washed over her in a flash flood of release.

Dan hauled her to the carpet as she fell limp over him.
She stretched out on her back, her grapefruits, fitted
snugly into her sturdy cotton bra, rock hard under his
nose.

He stretched out at her side. "We gotta get rid of the
citrus."

Joy cooperatively tipped toward him as he reached
back to unsnap the bra. The round yellow fruits
bounced out of the cups and rolled off in different directions. Nose-to-nose like bookends on the soft blue
carpet, they laughed over the sight.

"Can't let those grapefruits get away," she cautioned, stroking the solid plane of his hip.

He released a husky groan. "How far can they go?"

"How far will you let *me* go?" she returned in sultry
challenge. Before he could reply, Joy gave him a sudden shove. He toppled flat on his back.

"This is the way I like my men," she purred, crawl-
ing closer. "Down and ready." Like a soft kitten she
pounced, lavishing his throat, his chest with strokes and
kisses, moving lower to satisfy him as he had her.

When he could take no more, he snaked a hand
through her hair and drew her against his length. Joy's
eyes fluttered open dazedly. His eyes were midnight-
blue intense—with yearning, with anticipation.

She caught her breath as he slid into her.

"Feels so right . . ." He glided in and out, then back
in, savoring the tight contracting lock she had on him.

With noises of pleasure they seized the moment like
a runaway train. Rocking together in heart-pounding
rhythm until their skin glistened.

"Maybe we should slide those bolts on the doors and
forget the party," Dan suggested a short time later as he

huffed to his feet. "Just keep on loving each other over and over again."

Joy, sitting cross-legged on the floor, flashed him a naughty look. "Wouldn't that give new meaning to the term *party animal!* I wonder... Can I trust you in a quick shower?"

Dan grasped her arms and tugged her up. "Let's find out...."

10

Thrashing through the snow

"HERE'S A LADY I WANT to meet!"

Joy's back was to the kitchen doorway, but she recognized Gwen's voice immediately over the party din drifting from the front of the house. She set one last cookie on the silver tray before her on the counter, then turned with a sedate smile. "You must be Dan's sister, Gwen," she greeted in a deep maternal voice. "I'm Sister Constance Clarence, Dan's houseguest and kitchen helper."

"And a mighty fine helper she is," Mrs. Nettel interjected with pleasure as she removed a tray of canapés from the oven. "The cat's."

"I hope you're not scolding me, Mrs. N.," Gwen said on a laugh as she crossed the kitchen floor in Joy's direction. "I know I promised to help you, but William has been entertaining everyone at the piano."

"There are plenty of hands already," Mrs. Nettel replied briskly. "Dan needn't have hired so many helpers."

Joy and Gwen exchanged a brief, knowing look. Mrs. Nettel considered this party her territory.

"Hiring college students to serve is a tradition I started years ago, Mrs. N.," Gwen confessed.

"Humph!"

"So pleased to finally meet you, Sister," Gwen went on graciously, firmly clasping Joy's hand.

"Dan has told me all about you, Gwen."

Although Gwen was a pain in the ass when it came to social protocol, Joy had to admit she was spunky and attractive. Gwen didn't hunch in an effort to distort her height. She held her head high and wore spike heels. She looked especially striking tonight, with her dark gleaming hair captured in a pearl clip, and dressed in a drop-dead slim green tunic with transparent sleeves. Simple gold pieces encircled her throat and wrist. It was a look Joy would have liked to wear, had she been able to step out of character.

"So nice that you could spend the holidays here with him," Gwen was commenting, her wide red smile genuine. "Dan needs to be drawn into the spirit of the season." She paused, wagging a long manicured finger at her. "You know, there's something unique about you...."

Joy's eyes shifted behind her clear lenses. Had Gwen spotted a trace of the real Joy under the disguise?

"Something quite wonderful, something hopeful," Gwen enthused innocuously, to Joy's relief. "Has anyone ever told you that you have a natural cheeriness in your demeanor?"

Joy smiled, humbly gazing down at her black rubber-soled shoes. "It's been said," she modestly confessed. Gwen was going to blow up like an atomic bomb when she found out she was massaging the ego of the wild Bohemian Joy Jones!

"She's a saint," Mrs. Nettel declared, thumping a tray down on the table as a pretty young student in a black uniform innocently invaded her turf.

"You're too kind, Mrs. Nettel," Joy demurred. The neighbor lady was so controlling of her environment, so loyal to those she cared for. If she cared for Theo, they were in a lot of trouble....

"I see you're arranging my spritz cookies on a platter," Gwen observed with pride.

"Why, yes." Joy wrung her hands together, feeling like she was suddenly part of one of those instant-coffee-switch commercials. Would Gwen detect a difference? So far, so good. Gwen didn't notice any visual disparity. But taste... Joy cringed as Gwen plucked a doughy star off the platter and popped it into her mouth.

Gwen closed her eyes with a savoring sound. "Mmm, nothing like real butter cookies."

Joy beamed. "I couldn't agree more."

"I told Dan to share these with you during your stay," she said with a swallow. "He did, didn't he?"

"Well, to tell you the truth, Gwen, I helped myself. Couldn't resist."

Gwen's gaze fell to Joy's grapefruit bosom and foam-padded hips. "We all have our vices," she chirped.

Joy smiled back through gritted teeth. Gwen was insinuating that Sister Constance Clarence was fat! She most certainly was not. Just a little on the plump side.

Dan entered the room just as Joy was struggling for a pious, yet worthy comeback.

"So this is where the action is," he said, gauging the climate with keen blue eyes.

Joy gave him a small feline smile to ease his mind. The boyish grin he drew in return made her heart jump.

"I was just making Sister feel at home," Gwen assured, taking a second cookie.

Dan torturously watched Gwen's consumption of the spritz in much the same way Joy had.

"Simply yum," Gwen judged, taking a stemmed glass of champagne from the table.

Joy and Dan exchanged a proud conspiratorial look. They'd saved the day.

"So, what is my William up to now?" Gwen asked, aglow like a teenager.

"Still pounding away like a saloon keeper on my cherished Steinway grand," Dan grumbled, pouring himself a glass of champagne at the table.

"You promised to be good," Gwen pleaded.

"I'm always gracious to my guests," he declared. "Just ask the Sister, here." Dan smirked as Joy's cheeks tinted pink. Gwen clucked with disgust, checking her lipstick in the mirror beside the back door. "I wouldn't dream of asking Sister to tattle on you!"

"The perfect gentleman," Joy intoned.

"Most certainly," Mrs. Nettel added righteously, removing another container of food from the fridge.

"By the way, is Rex coming tonight?" Gwen asked abruptly. "He's usually right on the button for all your parties, dressed in one of those loud outfits of his, digging into the food like a ravenous animal."

"Perhaps he's on an assignment," Joy hastened to speculate, as Dan's face grew thunderous. The poor guy was going nuts wondering who was working against him.

"I sincerely hope he shows," Dan retorted with tense resolve.

Gwen's green sheath shimmered as she shrugged. "Well, Rex or no Rex, it's time we got back to the guests we do have."

"We'll be there in a few minutes," Dan said, stalling.

"No, no, no." Gwen dodged between the pair, grabbing elbows. "It's rude for us as hosts, Dan, to hide out in the kitchen. And it's a crime not to share Sister with the others."

Joy cooperatively moved along with the pair. Hopefully social crimes were the only ones on Gwen's mind.

The moment he entered the living room, Dan noticed that the background music had a more polished sound. As it should. The woman who'd taken over Harris's spot at the ebony grand was a Supreme Court justice who occasionally sat in with the St. Paul Chamber Orchestra. William Harris was by the buffet table, plunking tidbits into his mouth. With his chest puffed and a strut in his step, he reminded Dan of a peacock. The moment the prosecutor spotted the trio, he advanced.

"Why, darling, I thought you'd taken a powder," he said heartily to Gwen. "To the powder room!" He gave Dan a slap on the back and his lady a peck on the cheek.

"William, I'd like you to meet Sister Constance Clarence of the Goodwill Missions Worldwide," Gwen said in glowing introduction.

"Pleased, I'm sure, Sister."

Joy shook his hand, meeting his gaze steadily, blankly. Fooling all these people who knew her at trial time gave her a rush, made her long for regular audiences all the more. She just couldn't shake Mrs. Nettel's TV deal from her mind. Right now, however, the odds of it working out seemed slim.

"I hear you're writing a book on the Jerome Berkley murder trial, Mr. Harris," Joy commented lightly under the latter's curious scrutiny.

"Why, yes, Sister," Harris affirmed with pleasure. "You know of the case?"

"It made the national headlines," Joy said.

Dan felt Joy was playing with fire and flashed her a displeased look. Harris took note and promptly misconstrued the message.

"The book is not a popular subject with your benefactor, Sister. Sour grapes, pure and simple."

"In principle, there is nothing wrong with chronicling the Berkley case," Dan allowed, struggling to keep his tone level. "True crime can be informative and educational."

"Lucrative is the key word here," Harris bluntly corrected. "I'm the first to tackle the project and intend to reap big rewards."

"Had I wanted to write the book, I would've done so!" Dan hooted, shaking Gwen's hand from his sleeve. "And while we're on the subject, I believe it was a dirty trick to put Gwen in the middle, forcing her to cover for you."

Joy studied Dan with concern. It wasn't like him to lose control. First, at the mere mention of Rex. Now with William Harris. Of course, she felt responsible, being the one who dredged up his feelings, drawing them to the surface. Perhaps expressing oneself openly should be a gradual process for a man who'd lived privately for three decades. Considering the stress he was under, he was a loose cannon for anyone crossing his path tonight!

"And I think the secrecy surrounding the project is strange," Dan continued, smiling stiffly at some guests passing by.

"I didn't tell you about the book, because I didn't want you to think I was upstaging you personally and privately in one fell swoop," Harris confided on a low note.

Dan's brows drew to raven's wings. "Privately?"

"My engagement to Gwen," Harris clarified. "Been planning to pop the question now at Christmastime for several weeks. Finally did so last night. Knew you'd need time to handle it, Dan. After all, we will probably be moving out west. To California. Plan to start a private practice there, once my book makes its mark."

"I was going to tell you tonight myself, Dan," Gwen interposed nervously.

"Don't you worry about all your quaint sister-brother traditions, Dan. We'll fly back for this little shindig here each and every year." Harris looked over the crowd with bright eyes. "Mingling with these power players makes this man weak in the knees."

Dan was tempted to knock him to his knees! Then he felt Joy's hand over his clenched fist. Her touch was so soothing, as though she were holding him in her arms. Now there was more change to accept. Some of it was bound to be unpleasant from his point of view.

"Congratulations to you both," he offered with effort.

"Thank you, Dan," Gwen said, pleased.

"Dan was going to introduce me around," Joy interceded. "If you two will excuse us . . ."

"Thanks, honey," he said on a sigh as she drew him into a corner. "Talk about a tough moment."

"Gwen is a big girl who knows her own mind," Joy pointed out. Her hand was halfway up to his face when she yanked it back down to her side. This chaste role was the worst!

"I know Gwen's an adult," he said, smiling briefly over her near mistake. "And I'd like nothing better than to see her settle down and start Christmas traditions of her own. Heaven knows, we'll be doing it ourselves."

Joy gazed up at him with shining eyes. "We will?"

"Of course. It's obvious that Gwen and I no longer need to lean so heavily on one another for support. She's ready to move ahead just as I am. But her choice in mates—"

"It's her choice to make," Joy cut in softly.

"Yeah," he conceded. "Let's make the rounds. This may be your last chance to meet all of these 'power players.' As nice as they are, I believe next year's festivities will be done on a much smaller scale."

Joy was an instant hit among politicians and socialites alike. Of course, she knew there was an automatic respect for her habit, but they drew her into their discussions, delighted in her opinions. And so many remarked on the homey tree Dan had chosen this year. So inventive and personal, they said. She'd never had him over such a deep barrel before! She was so grateful that he hadn't replaced her tree with a fancier one. All he'd done was take down some of the ornaments that caused him the most pain. Starting next year, there would be new decorations to collect, new memories to build on.

The annual and final Burke reception was winding down to a pleasant end around one in the morning.

Then Rex showed up.

"Ho-ho-ho!" The tardy guest ambled into the living room decked out for action in a scarlet sports jacket, crisp green shirt, and a pair of tight black jeans.

If he had a black heart, he was putting up one hell of a jovial front, Joy mused, watching him from the shelter of the dining-room archway.

Murmurs of good cheer were returned by what was left of the sedate crowd, many of whom were quite accustomed to Rex.

Dan, engaged in a lively conversation with a congressman from Maryland concerning the Super Bowl play-offs, glanced at his watch. Rex joined the pair and Dan forced himself to make introductions. The moment the congressman moved on, Dan pounced on his partner. "So where the hell have you been?"

Rex reared back his head, an angled sheet of blond hair flapping in his eyes. "Gee whiz, Daddy-O. My curfew expired or what?"

"This thing is almost over," Dan persisted.

"I had a date," he replied easily, finger-combing back his hair. "One who doesn't mix well with blue-haired ladies and men who own their tuxedos."

"I see." Dan gritted his teeth, determined to confront him about the investigator in Florida.

"Hey, I heard the wildest thing while I was hanging up my coat, Danny," he intimated after a sip of the bubbly. "That you got a nun here tonight."

"Christmas is full of surprises," Dan commented.

"Yeah, but a—" Rex's square jaw slackened as Joy stepped into the room with a silver tray of steaming coffee cups.

"Sister Constance Clarence of the Goodwill Missions Worldwide," Dan announced, enjoying Rex's amazement. It was tough to usurp his savvy partner on the subject of females. And this was a doozy of a female!

Rex swiftly composed himself. "Oh, I get it," he crowed. "She's hired help."

"The college students left with the majority of the guests," Dan informed him. "She is just filling in as a courtesy."

"She came here with one of the blue hairs, then," he amended.

"No, Rex, she did not."

"Then what is the answer, man?" Rex snapped impatiently.

"She's my houseguest for the holidays."

Rex's mouth hung open. "You and her. Here. Have you flipped your lid?"

"Probably." Dan regarded him intensely. "Though I might ask the same question of you."

"What sort of crack is that?" Rex demanded in surprise.

"I got a call for you at the station yesterday, partner," Dan cut in angrily. "I did a little checking and discovered your sideline investigation."

"You've been nosing around in my business?" Rex growled under his breath. "What a rotten—"

"Dan!" Gwen hailed him from the foyer. "The Frys and Spensers are leaving. Oh. Hello, Rex," she added in merry recognition.

Rex lifted his glass in her direction. "Cheers, baby."

"I'll be right back," Dan told him curtly before striding off.

Dan ushered out the last of the guests before he dared hunt down Rex again. He was wise enough to know he was about to blow. Like a bursting dam. Like a plugged cannon. Like the last soldier holding down the fort. What he didn't want to do was make a spectacle of himself in public, however. The Burkes were a dignified family. And more than anything, he wanted to uphold that image at this their last holiday reception.

In the end, Gwen, Joy, Mrs. Nettel and his champagne-swilling partner were clustered around the piano as Harris played a choppy medley of Christmas classics. No one noticed when Dan nudged Rex and motioned him out of the room. No one but Joy, who slipped away herself at the first opportunity.

Joy darted into the kitchen after them in her flowing black habit. Where were they? A chill in the air drew her to the window facing the backyard.

The sight of the jostling pair would have been comical under lighter circumstances—circumstances where friendship and loyalty weren't at stake.

"Oh, my stars . . ." Her gasp of dismay echoed in the spacious hollow kitchen.

"What is it, Sister?" Gwen joined her at the window.

"Why, I was just thinking how boyish and rambunctious Dan and his partner are, frolicking out in the snow like a couple of carefree youngsters," she improvised on a note of forced gaiety.

When the women looked back out, Rex swung out at Dan, hitting him under the chin. He lunged for Rex and together they did an awkward cha-cha on the icy sidewalk near the cellar door. Dan slipped and fell back into the snowbank, Rex toppling after him. Together they tussled. Red against black, rolling over one another on the white ground.

"I don't think this is a spirited joust between buddies," Gwen said.

"I'm sure it's harmless enough," Joy desperately argued.

"This isn't like Dan at all, Sister," Gwen insisted. "Something is amiss...."

Meanwhile, outside, Rex was echoing Gwen's confusion.

"What's come over you, man?" Rex huffed as Dan rose to his knees, seizing him by the scarlet lapels. "Whatever it is, don't take it out on my threads. This jacket cost me three hundred bucks!"

"You're kidding!" Dan stopped, momentarily aghast over the news.

"Since when have I ever lied to you!"

With a fierce growl Dan lunged at him again, grinding his face into the crusty snow.

"I had better go out there," Joy announced, as Mrs. Nettel and William Harris trotted into the kitchen.

"No, Sister," Gwen protested with a detaining grasp. "You are too delicate, too refined to interfere in such a disgusting display."

Joy brushed past her, causing Gwen to gasp in dismay. "Sister, you mustn't! Let William—"

Joy slammed the back door shut after herself, stomping down the steps in her sensible shoes. They didn't even see her coming as they rolled over each other with grunts and oaths.

"Stop it, you idiots!" she hollered into the night, grabbing Dan from behind by the shoulders. The ringing in his ears distorted her command and assuming she was Rex, he bucked her off into the air. With a wild yelp Rex reached out in an effort to buffer her landing. Un-

fortunately he managed only to snag her long black veil
before she landed between them with an *umph*. Rex was
left holding the veil and a hairnet. Joy was left holding
the bag, as reams of her luxuriant hair spilled out on the
snow like a golden fan.

"So it is you!" Rex deduced jubilantly. "Joy to the
world! Danny is saved, after all!"

Joy lay still, gazing up into the velvet heavens with
glazed eyes. Dan's face hovered overhead, his expression frightened and concerned as he removed her
crooked wire glasses.

"I didn't know it was you, honey," he croaked,
drawing a gentle hand to her forehead.

"You didn't know she was the nun?" Rex hooted.

"No, stupid, I didn't know she was on my back."

The others were streaming out the back door now.
"Joy Jones!" Gwen shrieked, pressing her hands to her
ears. "Oh, no! You can't be Sister Constance Clarence."

Joy sat up, dazedly examining the semicircle of faces
above her. Gwen, of course, was bonkers with fury.
William Harris stood beside her with a lofty smirk.
Mrs. Nettel set off the trio with a grumpy look.

"Why, you were the blonde in the bushes the other
night," Mrs. Nettel blurted out in amazement.

"The blonde? The bushes?" Gwen demanded.
"Shouldn't surprise me any, really. Joy Jones would try
anything, do anything to steal the show!"

"Shut up, Gwen," Dan barked, easing a protective
arm around Joy.

"Well, well. I never thought she'd come back here,"
Harris muttered half to himself. "Not to you, Dan."

"What is the meaning of all this?" Gwen persisted. She stomped her heel on the slick sidewalk, nearly losing her balance over the trio. Harris caught her clumsily. "She has made fools out of us," Gwen accused, looking a bit foolish herself with her fiancé's hands in her armpits.

"Joy's in disguise for her own protection, Gwen," Dan retorted. "There is no nun from the Goodwill Missions Worldwide."

Gwen gritted her teeth. "You've been nothing but trouble since day one, Joy Jones. First you tore Dan apart by seducing him during the trial. Then you tore him apart by leaving. And now, in finale, you've turned him against his loved ones, drawing him into some sort of circus."

"I'd like an explanation," William Harris interceded with a measure of professional steel. "Why on earth would Joy need further protection? The trial is long over and all of Berkley's associates out of the Laff Trak Comedy Club have been rounded up."

"Someone is still after me, William," Joy informed him on a wail. "And I want it to stop, I tell you! Stop right now!"

She shivered in the shelter of Dan's arms. Here were her potential enemies, hovering over her like a shroud. It all seemed like a bad dream—the threat of the stalker, the need for the charade. The end was near. One way or another.

A tear slipped out of her eye as she surveyed them one by one, ultimately focusing on Rex at her side. "I don't know anything that could harm any of you. Yet one of you saw my Christmas card here at Dan's and tracked

me down. Please leave me alone. I just want to go on
with my life."

"She shouldn't be here in your care, Dan," William
Harris protested. "You aren't running a safe house." He
then looked at Joy with a gentler attitude. "After the
trust we shared during the trial, I'm puzzled as to why
you turned to the detective in your hour of need. If you
have problems, I can best handle them through my office. As a matter of fact, I suggest you gather your
things and come with me now."

Joy huddled against Dan's chest. "I'm finished with
the bureaucracy of the system, William. And with Theo
Nelson. In short, I've had it with the whole Berkley
trial. I am not a data bank full of damaging information. If any of you fear my photographic memory,
you're being just plain stupid! If you think I have the
money Theo Nelson got for his false alibi, forget it.
Only Theo knows where it is. And he isn't talking."

"You approached Theo Nelson without consulting
the D.A.'s office?" William Harris demanded.

"You visited him for your book," Dan cut in.

"Nelson tell you that?"

"I told Dan, William," Gwen interceded with reluctance.

Harris's features smoldered. "Oh, I see. Little brother
still leaning on you for everything."

"Not everything," Dan growled, curling his fist at his
side.

Harris turned back to Joy. "If Theo is up to further
no good, I would like fair warning. Did he tell you
anything useful?"

Joy glanced at Dan who shot her a warning look. "Not really. We talked about my career plans, and how he ended up in jail—via the high-speed chase."

"The hypocritical coward," Harris grumbled. "Holding a gun in one hand and a saint in the other, hoping to save both his hide and soul."

"Surely you don't think Joy is in cahoots with Theo Nelson?" Dan challenged, his temple throbbing dangerously.

Harris kept his eyes on Joy. "Running off as you did made you look guilty," William Harris chastised, his charm slipping a bit. "But I discounted it," he hastily added. "You were a remarkable witness. One I'd gladly like to interview for my book."

"Blast that wretched book!" Dan thundered.

"So you've been hiding her here all along," Gwen said. "Why, Dan? What were you hoping to accomplish?"

Dan's chest heaved. "I hoped to track down Joy's stalker and at the same time keep her safe."

"Oh, sure!" Gwen fumed. "You couldn't even trust me, your big sister. And to even insinuate that any one of us— Well, I'm going home. Right this instant. You and Constance Nuisance can gaggle through Christmas alone!"

"We all need to talk, Gwen," Dan objected, reaching for the transparent sleeve of her dress.

"I am too damn mad right now!" she flared, yanking out of his grasp. "What will the guests here tonight think when they hear? They thought Sister Constance Clarence was a doll. A generous, loving nun."

"Joy's heart is just as big as Sister Constance Clarence's," Dan retorted. "And I don't happen to care what other people think. My focus is right here. On Joy. On you. On the people we call friends."

"Let her go, Danny," Joy interceded tiredly.

"Yes, Danny," Gwen echoed hotly. "You'd have to arrest me to stop me!"

His eyes narrowed to dark slits. "How tempting!"

"Thanks a lot!" Gwen cried brokenly. "This should've been the happiest Christmas of my life! I'm engaged to the man I love. I'm on the brink of moving in with him. You've made a mockery of it all, Dan! Disapproving of William's book. Launching Joy out on our party guests. If you were going to hide her, why didn't you go all the way and find her a room someplace?"

"What a mean thing to say!" Dan chastised.

"I'm feeling mean," Gwen returned with a sniff. "You obviously think we're all a bunch of criminals after your precious Joy. Well, I for one am insulted beyond belief."

"How could I avoid insulting you?" Dan challenged. "It was a no-win situation from the start. I either had to keep Joy in hiding, tiptoeing around for answers, or confide the problem to you and have you immediately flare up with self-righteous indignation." Dan lifted his shoulders. "What would you have done, Gwen, had it been Harris here in Joy's place?" When she opened her mouth, he cut in to clarify, "Don't forget that it had to be one of you who took the Christmas card. Used the information to track Joy. That much is indisputable. Whoever spoke to her landlord in Orlando, knew all about her from the card. And," he added, "that card is missing. I told you so that day at lunch."

"This is unbelievable, Danny," Rex uttered in amazement.

"I just don't get it," Gwen declared. "Did she confront the visitor?"

"The *stalker*," Dan clarified. As the cold night air swept over his face, he realized he was chilled to the bone. "If you want to know more, come inside and sit down by the fire. I dare you to stay. To hash this out."

"Not on your life!" Gwen huffed. "Come along, William. We'll see ourselves out."

"But Gwen, I feel I should stay," William Harris objected, slipping along behind her on the icy sidewalk.

"Forget about that damn book, for once!" she shouted over her shoulder, pounding up the steps in her spike heels.

Harris looked back at the group with a jabbing finger. "I'm in this until it's over, Dan."

"Yeah, yeah," he said, waving after him.

"I am going home too, Dan," Mrs. Nettel announced flatly. "I've had enough excitement for one night."

"Don't worry, Danny," Rex consoled as they marched for the house. "I'm going to stay. We'll break out the really good brandy and have a nice cozy fireside chat. All about loyalty and truth. About the rip in my beautiful jacket."

11

Joy to the world

DESPITE DAN'S OBJECTIONS, Gwen, William Harris and Mrs. Nettel went on their unmerry way. Rex, however, was more than happy to lope behind Dan into his study. Dan had just poured three snifters of brandy when Joy entered, dressed in his robe and sweat socks.

"You'll catch your death in those wet clothes," she scolded the pair.

"You'll catch something else, Rex, if you don't start talking," Dan threatened as he peeled off his suit jacket.

"Okay, okay, keep your shorts on," Rex began. "I forgive you for being the world's worst host tonight, by the by. And for misbehavin' a lot in general over the last few days." His bushy blond brows furrowed over his hawkish nose. "It's not nice to keep secrets from your partner. But there was always something about Joy that brought out the madman in you. Now that I look back—on the cookie break-in, the bent spoon, and the generally insane behavior—I should've known for sure." He removed his red jacket and inspected its tattered condition with a tsk of his tongue.

"Forget about that thing!" Dan snapped.

"Sure," he smoothly guaranteed. "Cut me a three-hundred-dollar check for it and we'll be square."

"Me, replace that eyesore?" Dan hooted. "I'll buy you a decent one in its place. Something you can wear with pride." He clenched his fists at his sides as he weighed another relevant issue. "Now, just how is it, that a guy on a detective's salary can blow three bills on a gypsy jacket? And a whole lot more on a Rolex?"

"What bent spoon?" Joy demanded.

"We'll discuss it later, Joy," Dan said evasively, closing the drapes against the colorful light display along the avenue. "This guy's not getting off the hook."

"I imagine he was wrestling with a spoonful of temptation," Rex told Joy.

"Oh, yeah," Joy recalled. "The pretend mistletoe morning. The bowl had no spoon...."

"Why, oh, why don't I ever have those kinds of breakfasts?" Rex wondered in mock lament.

"Dammit, Rex!" Dan growled.

"You deserve to be punished a little, Danny," Rex reprimanded. "The idea of suspecting me of betrayal digs deep. As it happens, I have a nest egg of fun money, which I used to buy the jacket. The Rolex...was a gift."

Dan anxiously paced around the chair Rex chose to slump into with his drink. "Inheritance?"

"Nope. I earned it."

"What connection do you have in Florida, Rex?"

Rex's chest heaved under his green shirt. "It's really none of your business, man. But under the circumstances..." He trailed off on a relenting note, as if mentally collecting the best reply.

"You better than anyone should understand my position," Dan challenged. "My entire focus has been on keeping Joy safe. I vowed to protect her and was willing to do whatever I had to do."

"It's been killing him, Rex," Joy broke in softly. "Please help us."

"I guess I understand," Rex conceded. "Relationships can get loony. Which brings me to my explanation, Danny," he said. "Actually, I've been drowning in my own personal affairs of late, and therefore missed the change of habit around here, so to speak."

Joy giggled over the pun, giddy from exhaustion and alcohol.

"You deny taking the Christmas card, then?"

"Absolutely!" Rex scoffed. "I've got my own cards from my own people, and I've got my own girl trouble."

"Seems hard to believe," Dan said warily. "Your bachelor life seems pretty cut-and-dried to me. And you rarely make reference to your family—"

"I'm thirty-five years old! I had a life before I became a policeman. Oh, don't scowl that way!" he chastised. "I've always been a law-abiding citizen. I, ah—just sort of reinvented myself about fifteen years ago."

"Nobody stretches out a story the way you do," Dan complained, pacing the room to relieve some of his frustration.

"All right. I was a famous pop star in my formative years," Rex confessed with a sardonic smile. "The kind the girls ripped clean of their clothing and hid in hotel stairwells to attack."

Dan spun on him in amazement, brandy sloshing over the rim of his glass onto his fingers.

"Explains his money supply," Joy broke in helpfully.

Rex leaned forward in his chair, his expression earnest. "It's true, I swear. And it's easy enough to prove."

Taking a breath, he launched into one of his old hit songs.

"I know that voice!" Joy exclaimed excitedly, bouncing on the leather cushion. "He's *Velvet!*"

"Velvet what?" Dan snapped impatiently.

"It was a singing duo," Joy explained. "They were the lovebirds of the seventies. They crooned romantic ballads that made every teenage girl across America weep with longing. Barry Manilow with a babe."

Dan rolled his eyes. "Gee whiz, how could I have missed it?"

"Are you serious? They had a pack of hit songs back then. Rex and Mandy Velvet."

"Actually, Joy, we had only four hits," Rex modestly corrected. "And we were only hot for a couple of years. Once it was over, I can tell you I was enormously grateful that people did buy the publicity hype about our last name being Velvet. I walked away with a new lease on life, away from the pop scene, the long, sprayed hair and sequined outfits." He shook his head sheepishly. "The photos look silly now. But back then, it was the rage."

"So you weren't married to Mandy," Joy probed anxiously.

"Yeah, we were really married. Under the name Cameron." Rex studied the amber liquid in his stout glass as though peering into a crystal ball. His tone was wistful when he continued. "It was a painful thing with Mandy and me. We really ran hot and cold. Then our star began to dim. I handled it all right, but Mandy was devastated. In the end, not only did people stop wondering if our name was really Velvet, they stopped wondering if we were breathing."

"Sounds rough," Joy murmured in empathy.

"Murder," Rex said. "Believe it or not, Danny, I craved some stability in my nomad existence. Being a cop was my boyhood dream. There's the thrill of uncertainty, of danger. Yet, I can go home at night and kick off my shoes, read the paper, knowing that no tabloid is spying on me. Being famous can be hell, man. There's no way to close the door on the public."

"What does all of this have to do with the private eye in Florida?" Dan prodded.

"Well, Mandy reinvented herself, you see—a few years after our divorce. Guess she had to survive in the business. You probably never heard of her, either, Amanda Germain is her—"

"Amanda Germain consorted with the likes of you?" Dan thundered in disbelief.

"Yeah," Rex said, bristling.

"She's a legend in pop music for cripes' sake!"

"Her dream come true. As it happens, she's based in Florida. She claimed to have gotten herself in a little trouble and asked me to help." Rex sighed. "Well, all sorts of warning alarms went off in my head at the thought of facing her. We were TNT together. It was bliss and torture." He shook his head, briefly immersed in his own world. "We got right off to a lousy start. She sent me the Rolex, as though I needed a bribe. I, in turn, hired a detective agency as a go-between."

"You were talking to her when Gwen walked in on you," Dan surmised.

"Right. You see, I seriously doubted she ever was in any trouble."

"So, is everything all right, Rex?" Joy asked softly.

His expression hardened. "No. It looks like I'll be taking some leave after the holidays to fly down there myself."

"Well, help yourself to a spoon or two," Dan invited with a wave. "I think you're going to be needing them."

"Yeah, I just might," he agreed. "You do understand now, don't you, Dan?" he queried anxiously. "The trust forged between us is so special, so necessary in our work."

"Yes, of course." Dan moved to Rex's chair to pat him on the shoulder. "I probably should've laid my cards on the table right off. But I've been running on pure desperation since Joy arrived. I just pulled in my flanks and hoped the answer would become clear." He grinned. "I can't tell you how relieved I am to have everything out in the open between us. And to discover that you can't always handle your wild women, either." Dan paused, waiting for Joy's rebuttal. When it didn't come he turned to find her fast asleep in the chair, her empty snifter in her lap.

Dan regarded her tenderly. "She was bound to crash."

"And so are we, partner," Rex murmured, rising to his feet. "Let's try and get some sleep ourselves. Look at this mess with a fresh eye tomorrow."

"Thanks, buddy." Dan extended his hand in friendship.

"We can do better," Rex said gruffly, giving him a big bear hug.

"I've never been so scared, Rex," Dan confessed, as he broke away with a grateful slap on the back. "Not even in our worst moments on the street."

"The personal slant weakens a guy's edge," Rex mused understandingly. "And Joy losing her veil has probably taken away the only trump card you had. Maybe we should bundle her up right now and whisk her out of here."

"It's officially Christmas Eve," Dan announced with a wistful look at his watch. "Spiriting her away while she sleeps would be too devastating a blow." Dan squeezed his eyes shut for a long moment. "Can I ask one last favor of the night, though?"

"I'll be glad to sleep on the sofa," Rex replied in swift telepathy. "Just give me a blanket, a pillow, and a rundown on everything you have so far."

The sharp ring of the telephone cut through the silence of the bedroom shortly before sunrise on Christmas Eve morning. Joy and Dan bolted up in bed simultaneously. As the second ring cut through the room, a man's silhouette loomed in the doorway.

"Dan!" Joy cried out, clinging to his shoulder. "It's a big old bear!"

"It's just me, Goldilocks," Rex retorted. He entered the room in Dan's gray sweatsuit, stubbing his toe on the dresser in the shadows.

Joy hastily rolled over to switch on the bedside lamp. "Oops, didn't know you were still around, Rex."

"I'll put it on the speaker," Dan decided, reaching past Joy to the telephone beside the lamp. "Hello. Burke."

"Dan?"

Dan met Rex's gaze with surprise. "Repeat?"

"Right. Can you talk?"

"Sure."

"I hate these speakers."

Dan decided to feign mild irritation and express only partial interest. "I'm in bed, man. What do you want?"

"Got fifty bucks to make this call."

Dan's exchange with Rex sharpened.

"From who?" Dan prodded.

"Don't know. Slipped a note under my door with the dough."

"What's the message?"

"Your front yard is decorated," he recited dubiously, obviously reading it off the note. "You get it?"

Dan's frown deepened. "My yard is the only one not decorated."

"Expensive prank." Repeat chuckled. "Easiest dough I made all year."

"Repeat—"

"I know, I know, save the note. But I can tell you it's a dead end. Scrap of paper, printed letters."

Joy pressed the disconnect button when the dial tone buzzed through the speaker.

"Could be a friend from the station," Rex wagered. "Some of the guys do tease you about your Castle, here. Your lack of decoration is common knowledge."

Dan shrugged. "Maybe someone hung a tiny wreath on the door or something."

"I know I can't sleep anymore," Joy proclaimed, flipping back the covers.

"It's only six o'clock," Rex protested.

Joy was already darting around the room, gathering her clothing. "You ought to be ashamed of yourself. You scared the heck out of me, standing there like a big old hulk!"

Rex shot her an amused look. "You ought to be ashamed, conking out on us last night. Like my life story put you to sleep."

"Boring, you're not, Velvet man!" She took her exit, in a whirlwind of blond hair and huffs of indignation. "I'll check for decorations," she called back in a fading voice.

"Don't go outside," Dan warned. "We'll be right down."

"You've got to stop her from calling me Velvet, Danny," Rex beseeched in mortification. "I've kept that secret for fifteen years!"

"I'll speak to her," Dan replied, unable to mask a flicker of amusement.

"Show her who's boss!" Rex advised, agitation twitching his jaw.

"Easier said than done," Dan complained, hopping out of bed. "Females like Joy aren't especially easy to tame."

"Amanda was in that league, too," Rex confessed on a sigh. "Cured this tigress-tamer. Give me a pliable one every time."

"But you're flying back to her," Dan teased as he pulled fresh underwear from his drawer.

Rex gawked at the cotton briefs. "Those undies ironed?"

"Mrs. Nettel," he affirmed, stepping into them.

"That dame is spooky, I tell ya!" Rex raked a hand through his light hair as he dropped down on the edge of the bed.

"She'd be a jewel if she were yours," Dan retorted, easing on a bright plaid flannel shirt.

"The question is, why is she yours, Dan? You don't pay her a fortune. You didn't save her life. And her behavior around this house is obsessive."

"She likes me."

"So does Joy, but she'll never iron your jocks, man." Dan shot him a dirty look as he zipped up his creased blue jeans. "I'd rather not lose either lady," he confessed.

"Maybe you won't have to," Rex said. "This situation just needs a dose of objectivity, is all."

"Objectivity," he pondered mockingly. "Seems I've forgotten the meaning of the word."

"It can't be that bad."

"Oh, no? Number one on my agenda is a visit to Gwen's. For the first time in my life I'm not certain I know where she stands. On anything!"

Rex nodded in understanding. "In the meantime I'll do a little digging on the elusive Mrs. Nettel."

Dan grimaced in frustration. "I feel the answer is in front of my face and I can't quite clearly make it out."

"Relax, it'll come."

"If only I had Joy's photographic memory. I'd be the Sherlock Holmes of the Twin Cities!"

The men tramped down the stairs, further speculating on Repeat's call.

"Joy, we're going outside for a minute," Rex announced in the empty foyer.

"She *is* outside," Dan growled, catching sight of her in the front yard through the narrow front window. During the short time that he'd been dressing, Joy had ferreted out a shovel from the kitchen utility closet, bundled up in one of his down jackets, a knit cap and gloves, and barreled into the dawn to scrape away some macabre-looking message spray-painted in red on the snow-covered lawn. "So Repeat *did* have something."

Rex took his place at the window as Dan darted to the closet for outerwear. "You know what it says?"

Dan spared him a glance as he eased into his green parka. "Didn't make it out."

"Killjoy."

"Dammit!" Dan struggled to shove his feet into his boots.

"There's a guy running up the street with something in his hands!" Rex shouted, yanking open the door. Dan shot out to find it was George Maynard coming to the rescue with a shovel of his own.

"Morning, Detective," he called out. "Saw you had a prankster at work."

"Yes," Dan said tersely, flashing him a grateful smile. Joy grasped his arm, her face flushed and distraught. "Can't let the kids see this, Danny."

"You are so beautiful, honey," he whispered.

"Saw the Sister out here working," George went on, digging into the red snow. "She's been so good to my Cindy and Tommy.... Just want to repay the kindness."

Dan watched for a brief moment as Joy scooped into the snow and followed the neighbor to the street. Mrs. Nettel hadn't blown the whistle on Sister Constance Clarence yet. A kindness or part of the game?

"I hope there isn't an ordinance against dumping this stuff out here," the neighbor called back over his shoulder.

"Wouldn't know," Dan lied in return.

A light flicked on across the street, and Jane Weaver's husband came clopping over to help. A few minutes later Rex returned in a jacket, carrying two more shovels. There was a lot to like about these people, Dan was coming to realize. As gradually as the passage of seasons, he was beginning to see just how wonderful change could be. It had been a long time since he'd experienced personal growth, and it felt as invigorating as the brisk winter air. All because of Joy. Oh, how he hated to send her away again. But he really had no other choice.

"THAT WAS A DIRECT threat on your life," Dan reiterated an hour later as he drained his orange juice at the kitchen sink, methodically rinsing his cup.

Joy rushed up to him, huddling close. "But I want to be with you!"

Dan cupped her face in his hands. "You will be. I just need to speak to Gwen alone. Get some things straight. Rex will be your stand-in bodyguard for a couple of hours."

"We're trying to save your Christmas, dopey," Rex informed her with a nudge between the shoulder blades.

"What about tonight, Danny?" she grilled, burying her face in his shirt. "We'll be here together, won't we?"

Dan pinched her chin and tipped up her face. "I'm going to be straight with you. Rex is taking you out of here in a little while—"

Her eyes blazed liquid green fire. "No! I'm not budging!"

"He's taking you to Metro Station while he does extensive background work on Mrs. Nettel. I'll meet up with you there and hopefully by then we'll have some answers."

"Then we'll come back here," she told him.

"Not unless I have my hand on your stalker's collar," Dan stated firmly.

"Our Christmas will be ruined again."

"I'm frantically trying to save this Christmas for us," Dan insisted.

"You could save our Christmas without any fuss at all," Joy cajoled, running her fingers over the soft fabric of his flannel shirt. "Just lock the doors and slide the bolts into place. Turn the music up and the lights down...."

"I can't," Dan replied in anguish. "It just wouldn't be right."

Joy read the perplexity underneath the sympathy and realized that he truly didn't understand how she could suggest such a thing. So much for progress. Dan was the same old dictator. First sign of discomfort and he was filing her away again. "All right," she eventually said on a sigh. "I know when I'm licked."

Dan had no notion of just how weighted her final surrender was. When she left with Rex fifteen minutes later, her leather waist sack, full of her getaway belongings, was cinched over the waistband of her jeans, concealed beneath a roomy blue sweater. Hardly the appropriate attire for air travel, but it would have to do. She'd called Mr. Sheldon from the bedroom and he was making arrangements for her ticket to Florida on his end with a credit card. All she had to do was make the flight....

12

Comin' down my chimney tonight

"I AM SO MAD AT YOU, Dan!" Gwen shot her brother a condemning look as he crossed the threshold of her suburban town house. "And wipe those feet before you take another step!"

Dan obliged, but his feet were the last thing on his mind. Disconcerting images of Joy's broken expression kept creeping into his vision. He'd failed, as both Santa and bodyguard. He wandered into the sunny living room and sank into the center of Gwen's sectional couch with a sigh.

Gwen, dressed in a flowing housecoat, flounced across the carpet to shut off the television. Her green satin hem took flight as she turned to assail him. "So, what are you doing here?"

Dan gazed up at her stormy figure with cool levity. "We have to talk."

Her blue eyes blazed. "I think not!"

"Sit down." His tone was on the border of lethal. She dropped into a chair with a flicker of shock.

"Your treatment of me has been horrible." She pursed her lips and knees primly together, clasping her hands in her lap.

"Gwen, I'd hoped this conversation would never evolve, but I need answers. Fast."

"The way you flaunted Joy under your roof as a nun was disgraceful!"

"No, Gwenny. The way I fell for Joy, the way I kept her arrival from you—those are the things that annoy you."

"Of course, they do!" she snapped back. "What am I to make of it all?"

"I've felt obligated to shield Joy from the world for a host of reasons." When Gwen began to grumble back, he cut her off. "Joy was an important witness in a serious case. A stalker has gone to a great deal of trouble to track her cross-country. I am the man who was selected to protect her from the start. As a dedicated cop, I would feel—no matter who the witness happened to be—an obligation to see this through."

Gwen's thin dark brows arched under his hard look. "You act as though I'm somehow responsible."

"Do you resent me, Gwen?" he asked suddenly. "Have I held you back, spoiled your holidays over the years?"

Gwen gasped in dismay. "Is that what you think, Dan?"

Dan swallowed hard, pushing back the emotions climbing in his throat. "I don't know anymore. And William Harris has been flapping off about it. I just want a straight answer from you."

"The idea is ridiculous!" she cried with a swing of her shiny black head. "I admit that William has gone overboard with his criticism. You certainly bring out the competitor in him, personally and professionally. And perhaps I've let some of his opinions sway me because I love him. But I will set him right on the way things are

with us." Gwen sighed hard. "You are my precious little brother, silly. I only want to help you."

Dan nodded, only partially appeased. "Let's say you
don't wish to punish me at all, then."

"Not yet, anyway. . ." She trailed off under his agi-
tated look.

"Let's say you've been trying to help me out, as you
always have in the mother-hen mode. That you decided to do something about Joy. Track her down, for
instance, force her back into my arms with scare tac-
tics. The Christmas card would've made that easy."

"Digging up Joy Jones never occurred to me," she said
in disbelief. "So this train of logic is useless."

Dan beamed in relief as he rose to his feet. "I'm glad
to hear it. And I will try to get used to William. Looks
like he'll be a family fixture from now on, with your
forthcoming marriage."

"The perfect gift for me this year!" Gwen shot up to
give him a hug.

"Then I'll return the gift I bought you," he teased,
tweaking her nose.

"Don't you dare!"

"Well, I have to go," he announced, releasing her.
"Rex is looking out for Joy, and doing a thorough check
on Mrs. Nettel. She must have taken the card. There is
no one else."

Gwen raised her eyes to his. "Uh, Dan?"

His gaze sharpened over her meek expression.
"What?"

"Has it occurred to you that the person who took the
card is completely innocent of everything else?"

"No."

"Well, I did and I am."

Dan's face burned red. "So you had it all along!"

"I acted out of love for you, not hate for Joy. I caught you mooning over it on Saturday and just stuffed it in my purse. And William agreed that it was best."

"Harris did see the card, then?"

"Well, yes. He was the one who threw it into the fire. As I said before, I wouldn't have gone looking for that girl."

But William Harris might have. All on his own. "I've got to go," he announced abruptly.

"I'll be seeing you tonight, tomorrow," she called after him hopefully.

"Don't speak to anyone about this conversation, Gwen," he told her. "It's the least you can do."

She followed him to the door. "All right. I love you, you know."

Dan smiled wanly at his meddling sibling. "Merry Christmas, Gwenny."

DOWNTOWN ST. PAUL WAS heavy with Christmas shoppers. Dan maneuvered his unmarked sedan down the tangle of narrow streets near the cathedral, creeping up on Metro Station from behind. Rex was hanging up the telephone just as Dan entered their office.

"Just calling Gwen's in search of you," Rex informed him.

Dan perused the small square room, then took a sidelong look down the hall. "Joy in the bathroom? Down in the cafeteria? Where?"

Rex's face fell. "I lost her, man."

"Impossible!" Dan roared, throwing his arms into the air. "It's only been an hour and a half!"

"She had a plan, okay?" Rex planted his hands on the desktop and rose to his feet. "Spilled a dab of soda pop on her sweater and trotted off to the john. Looking back, I know it was a ruse."

Dan swore under his breath. "I should've seen it coming."

"I've got more bad news," Rex continued. "I worked on the hunch that Mrs. Nettel might be a registered CPA. It got me on the right scent. Turns out her name is Shirley Nelson, Theo's sister."

"Blast!"

Rex nodded soberly. "Yeah. Nobody knows better than you how protective sisters can be. It's a miracle she didn't string you up in your own cellar."

"Gwen is the one who stole Joy's Christmas card from my house," Dan interjected.

"You think she's clean, don't you?"

Dan nodded. "But William Harris saw it at her place."

"The walls are closing in. We've got to locate Joy."

Dan rubbed his temples. "Where to start?"

"Put yourself in her place, Danny."

"I can't!" Dan lamented. "It's too big a reach for me. But you can, Rex," he said urgently. "You're a dizzy blonde yourself."

"Well, if it were me," Rex mused, "I'd be so hoppin' mad, so needy for strokes, that I'd seek out the coziest, second-best Christmas I could think of."

"Yes!" Dan rejoiced. "You're a genius. I think." He sat on the edge of the desk and turned the telephone around to face him. "A quick call to the airlines to check the Orlando flights and one to the telephone company to check my long-distance records."

"Why don't you just call the Sheldons?" Rex suggested.

"Because I don't want Joy to run again."

THE FIRST THING JOY SAW when she disembarked the plane at the airport in Orlando was Henry Sheldon and Alice, his missus. She'd warned them that she would be arriving sans her red wig, so they instantly recognized her.

"I could've taken a cab," she said, running over to them.

"Nonsense!" Mr. Sheldon scoffed, his round face flushed and merry.

"We're so relieved you're all right," Mrs. Sheldon lilted, embracing her. Petite like Joy, with fading blond hair, the older lady could easily have been mistaken for Joy's mother. "And you're just in time to celebrate Christmas Eve. I was just wrapping some small toys for the neighborhood children when you called."

"Yup, looks like I got my elfin helper, after all," Mr. Sheldon bellowed cheerily. "Any luggage to retrieve?"

"Not a thing," Joy replied, blinking back the tears. They were so dear, so anxious to help.

"Of course, your things are ready and waiting back home, just as you left them, Faye. And your car is safely back in the garage."

"I have so much to tell you," Joy said with a sniff as they sandwiched her between them. "Starting with who I really am and what brought me here the first time around."

"Wonderful," Henry Sheldon boomed. "The missus loves a good story."

Joy spent part of the afternoon decorating the apartment house's community party room. The rectangular basement room had windows facing the street in front, and Joy frequently found herself gazing through the glass at the traffic and pedestrians with a measure of fear and longing. She'd begun to regret her impulsive escape. Dan would be worried sick. But he deserved it, didn't he? Her emotions were on a seesaw. He had tried so hard to make it right for her. But he was so bullheaded, once he made a choice. It was an hour earlier in Minnesota. Close to dinnertime. Was Dan sitting by their old spindly tree all alone?

DAN WAS USING EVERY moment to his advantage, the wonders of the holiday far from his conscious mind. He had easily confirmed the call to Sheldon from his home phone, and the airline reservation made by him for one Faye Fairway. The airlines confirmed that the flight had landed on time forty-five minutes ago. A flight attendant remembered Faye/Joy quite well, because she sniffled her way across the country. Dan would dry those tears himself, he vowed. And never let her out of his sight again.

All the while he worried over the facts. What was it that didn't jibe? There'd been something. His instincts told him so.

Rex barged into the office with sandwiches and milk as Dan was thumbing through his wallet. "What's the plan?"

"Well, I'm off to Orlando. You want to come?"

Rex's eyes lit up. "Try and stop me."

"I have to stop home and collect a credit card, some cash. And I believe I'll have a word with Mrs. Nettel, as well."

"Think there's time?" Rex questioned.

"Flight leaves in ninety minutes. Plenty of time."

Rex flashed him a doubtful look. "That's shaving it pretty close. Maybe we should drive to the airport separately. Just to guarantee that one of us makes it."

Dan was a bit surprised. "I'll make it. I just don't want to sit around the terminal when I could be using the time more efficiently."

"Is it the next Orlando flight out of here?" Rex asked.

"There's one in twenty minutes, but I can't possibly make that one."

Rex shrugged. "Well, I'll meet you at the Sheldons' place if we get separated. Proceed with caution, Danny. Shirley Nelson may be one twisted pretzel."

"Just seeing her in the flesh will put my mind at ease," Dan confided. "It will mean she didn't follow Joy down to Florida."

"Don't worry," Rex placated, stuffing a sandwich in his pocket as he headed for the door. "Somebody would've had to be damn close to pick up Joy's scent here at Metro."

AS THE CHRISTMAS PARTY in the Sheldons' apartment house swung into full gear that night, Joy couldn't help noticing how different it was from the swank crowd at Dan's. Of course, rambunctious children awaiting Santa's arrival were bound to add an aura of pandemonium to any gathering. But these people were a far more casual, less monied crowd, as well. And living near each other day after day, they shared a neighborly intimacy and warmth that couldn't be matched by mere social contacts.

Dan could have this camaraderie with his own neighbors, she fleetingly thought. If he went ahead and tore down his fences—inside and out.

Her costume at this party was a far cry from Sister Constance Clarence's flowing black habit, she thought, looking downward. It consisted of a skimpy red bolero jacket and miniskirt trimmed in fake white fur over white tights and turtleneck. Accented with only little black slippers and a belt it was certainly sunshine Christmas attire. A girl would freeze rock solid at the North Pole. Or in Minnesota. If a girl happened to be there as someone's own personal elf . . .

Joy bent over the punch bowl and dipped the ladle into the thick green sherbert concoction, only to feel a sharp nip on her lower cheek. "Eek!" She straightened with a squeak, dropping the ladle back into the bowl with a splash. She whirled around, rubbing her backside. "Okay, who's the wise guy?"

A cluster of young boys gaped at her in bewilderment. "A big boy says pinching elves makes Santa's sleigh come faster," a small redhead piped up, grinning toothily.

"And we don't mean Santa Sheldon, either," a second one squeaked excitedly.

"Definitely a false rumor," she halfheartedly scolded with a wagging finger.

Grumbles followed her reply.

"You're much better off helping Mrs. Sheldon with some of those cookie trays," she advised, turning back to the punch. A moment later something nudged her in the side. "Enough is—" She spun around again to find a heavily made-up Santa with a huge bushy beard and mustache crowding her against the table. This character certainly wasn't Henry Sheldon. And the nudge in her waistline wasn't a playful pinch.

It was the barrel of a gun—a small-caliber one that fit quite discreetly into Santa's gloved palm.

"Who..." Joy's mouth went chalky as she gasped for words.

"Move out of here," a raspy voice ordered. "Now." When Joy paused, Santa eyes slitted underneath his huge droopy white brows. "If I start shooting in here, somebody might get hurt. Save Christmas for the kiddies, comedy queen."

Joy obediently wove through the crowd, out the doorway, then up the short flight of stairs and out the front entrance. Despite the fact that it was still near the seventy-degree mark, a shiver raced down her spine, drawing goose bumps to her skin. Had anyone seen her leaving? Hopefully so. The Sheldons knew everything about her now. Any funny business and they'd have the cavalry here in minutes. If she could just stall this creep. "Look, I don't think you want to hurt me," Joy urged, attempting to reason. She tried to confront her assailant, only to have the gun jabbed into her spine.

She gritted her teeth in agony. "Ah, maybe you just don't want me to see you."

"It's for our mutual benefit that you don't."

This person desperately wanted to remain unidentified. So he or she could reappear in Dan's life without detection, no doubt! "Just tell me what you want," she coaxed.

"Your car," the voice hissed.

That was the last request she expected! "It's in the garage."

"It wasn't last week," the voice warily challenged. "And it isn't now."

This had to be the original stalker. The car had been missing when Pat Fairway made his original appearance. But why would anyone want that old beater? "My landlady drove it to Tampa," she calmly explained. "It's out there now, honest."

"Show me." The gun was at her jugular vein, and a heavy hand was on her arm, nudging her along. There was no chance for a diversion, since Santa knew where the garage was. She stumbled across the lawn, past the flowering bushes and the Santa robot, circling around to the back of the building.

The lock was broken on the service door leading to the multiple stalls. Joy hated like hell to be trapped in the dark confines of the brick building with this creature, but there was no choice. Producing the car was her best bet. Santa was welcome to it.

In spite of it all, she couldn't help thinking: Another Christmas down the tubes.

"C'mon, c'mon!" The ugly voice urged her on, as a mighty hand gave her a shove. Not once did the barrel of the gun leave her skin.

"There it is," she muttered, gesturing to the boxy old Plymouth at the end.

"Your car is green!"

"I had it painted brown."

Joy cried out as a gloved hand reached over her belly. Before her echo died away, she realized that it was her belt the Santa was after. Grabbing her mane of hair, Santa shoved her to her knees by one of the steel poles supporting the ceiling. "Put your wrists around the pole."

"No, please," she croaked.

"Do it!"

Joy cried out again as Santa's boot came down on her extended calf, sending an excruciating spasm through her tendons. Pressing her into the pole from behind, Santa grabbed her wrists and shackled her to the steel with her own velvet belt. Satisfied that she was properly restrained, Santa headed for her Plymouth and yanked open the driver's door and swore. Joy's heart pumped madly in her chest beneath her bolero jacket. Santa stormed back to her and pressed the gun against her temple.

"Where is the Saint Christopher statue?"

Joy's brain ticked through the fog of panic and pain. "What?"

"On the dashboard!" The boot dug into her leg again. "Is this really your old car?"

"Yes! It was there, it was there," she wailed, trembling in fear and pain. Tears streamed down her face. Who would want that little statue of the patron saint of travel?

"Think!"

"I don't know!"

A palm smacked her mouth, and the sharp edges of her front teeth slit her lip. "Don't get cute with me."

Joy's fragile emotions were just about spent, but to her blessed relief, she was lucid enough to replay Alice Sheldon's departure for Tampa in the car. The landlady had slid in behind the wheel, babbling on about Saint Christopher no longer being a saint. At the time, Joy had dismissed the incident as rather comical, especially after the way Theo Nelson had clung to the statue all through the chase with the police. Mrs. Sheldon had then reached over and removed the statue to make room for her travel mug. Joy pinched her hot, burning eyes shut. What did Alice do with it? "Glove, glove—"

"Glove compartment!" The boot was lifted. More clomping over the concrete floor.

This time the tone was triumphant. The Santa returned with the plastic statue. He'd loosened its cardboard bottom and extracted a wad of tissue. Obviously something had been hidden in the hollow center.

"Go away!" Joy cried, cowering against the pole. "Please!"

"Keys. To the car."

"Ah—ah, there used to be a set under the sun visor on the driver's side," she babbled before he could come any nearer.

The keys must've still been there, she reasoned, because the boots headed for the stall door in front of her Plymouth. She peeked out of the shelter of her arms to see the top of Santa's hat over the roof of a pickup truck as he heaved up the garage door, sending a waft of sweet ocean air inside. It would soon be over, she rationalized, trying to quell the bubbling hysteria surging through her system. If she didn't make a peep, maybe he would just leave. Hopefully the old junker would start up. It did! The engine wheezing to life was the sweetest sound of Christmas. The Plymouth's headlights flashed on, too! Joy rested her head against the pole, weeping quietly. The car was rolling out.

Then the brakes squealed. There were shouts outside. The clomping of boots. In the garage?

Santa ran back inside, but a hand was on his furry white collar. Dan's hand. He was there. Large as life, lifting the bogus Santa right off the ground in a fit of rage.

Joy inched her way to her feet, using the pole as leverage. "Dan!" She was sobbing uncontrollably as he spun to meet her eyes. With a violent ripping motion, he tore away Santa's hat and hair.

"You crummy bastard!" he roared. "I finally remembered your blooper on the plane coming down here!" He shoved William Harris into the arms of two uniformed Orlando officers and rushed for Joy. "Baby, baby..." He loosened the cloth belt at her wrists and she collapsed against him. He held her in the crook of his arm, inspecting her bloody mouth and bruised cheek in dismay.

"Better get her to a hospital right away," Rex advised from behind them.

"Yes, indeed," the Sheldons chimed in fretfully.

Joy shook her head. "No, no, I'm going to be fine." She buried her face in the softness of Dan's bright flannel shirt—the same shirt he'd put on this morning. What a dreadfully long day it had been. "There's just one thing I need to know right now, copper."

Dan gently kissed her temple. "What is it, Joy?"

"What took you so damn long?"

Epilogue

Troubles will be out of sight

"COMFY, HONEY?"

"Never better." Joy snuggled against Dan on the sofa, gazing out at their spindly evergreen overloaded with lights and ornaments. It was Christmas night and they'd miraculously managed to get back to the Burke Castle to see the holiday through. Save for some nasty bruises, Joy was rejuvenating quite nicely. Naturally her sense of humor was the first to return. Her curiosity over the loose ends was a close second. There were so many things to discuss.

"What a fella," Dan said in self-congratulation, rearranging the afghan on her legs. "I promised you a Pendham Avenue Christmas and you got one."

"The Fates allowed," she murmured dreamily.

"Yeah, right," he admitted with a chuckle. "But give me some credit for putting this fragmented puzzle together."

"I do, copper. They all cracked because of your determination. Who'd ever have guessed that William Harris was so desperate to interview Theo Nelson for his book, that he'd make a deal with him the way he did?"

"Theo must have been tied up in knots all year, stuck in prison, knowing that the safety-deposit key he'd hidden in your Saint Christopher statue might be lost forever. He couldn't even trick you into handing over the statue because you'd disappeared."

"Then along came William Harris with his book interview. Talk about the perfect homing pigeon. Who would be better equipped to track me down and produce the statue and the key?"

"A marriage of convenience between two desperate men," Dan declared. "Nelson desperate to recover the alibi payoff money hidden in the safety-deposit box at the bank. Harris desperate to make the big time with his book. Just imagine how angry cocky Harris was when he went to interview Nelson about the money-laundering operation at the Laff Trak, only to discover that there was an incredible string attached to Nelson's inside information."

"Yeah, that creepy beast, Theo," Joy muttered. "Taking me hostage in my own car, stashing his deposit-box key in my statue. I thought he was clutching Saint Christopher during the chase just because he was so scared."

"No, I don't think he's one to depend on a higher being for comfort," Dan said with a dry chuckle. "I imagine he was hedging his bets. If you got him away safely, he would've run with the statue. When you got caught, he just set it back on the dashboard for safekeeping. He had no way of knowing there would be stragglers in Jerome Berkley's network who were a threat to you. That you'd leave town. I imagine he planned to just ask for the statue as a gift. And being the softy you are, you'd have promptly delivered it."

"Well, you helped me to see Theo for what he is," Joy conceded.

"He sure maintained his cool about the money," Dan said in awe. "Steadfastly denied ever being paid off by Jerome Berkley for that alibi."

"Yeah. Then, when I went to see him all in a dither the other day, he acted like my old pal." Joy glowered. "I'll bet he couldn't wait to call Prosecutor William Harris to tell him I was back, that I still had my car stashed someplace."

"The car was everything," Dan affirmed. "Apparently Harris had tried to track you himself through channels."

"And would've found me, had I entered the Witness Protection Program as you wanted me to," Joy gibed.

"Yes," Dan admitted. He came up empty for a couple of months, according to his confession. You'd covered your tracks well. Until you sent the Christmas card to me. It was a windfall for Harris when Gwen brought it to her place. He had your return address! He got real busy, real fast, in an effort to produce the key for Nelson. First he checked out your apartment garage to no avail. Perhaps the car was out on the street someplace, was all he could figure. He had no way of knowing it was in Tampa with Alice Sheldon. So he posed as your cousin Pat Fairway for Mr. Sheldon's benefit, hoping to flush you out and into your car. He never intended to confront you—he didn't want to run the risk of being recognized. He just waited across the street for you

to return and discover a mysterious cousin had visited."

"Bet he nearly croaked when I left on foot," Joy interjected.

Dan nodded. "He had to return home a loser. In his
arrogance, however, he hoped you'd run to him for answers, if you came back here at all. He never suspected
you'd give me a second chance. Just doesn't understand my attraction to females, I guess," he teased.

"He, like everyone else, was fooled by my nun's disguise," Joy proudly reminded him.

"Right up to the moment when Rex pulled off your
veil. It must have really shook him, because that's when
he made his mistake. He referred to the Saint Christopher statue, to Theo holding it along with the gun during the chase. Well, we both know that didn't come to
light during the trial.

"He then attempted to scare you off once again in the
direction of the car. He sprayed 'Killjoy' on the snow
and hired Repeat to make the dramatic announce-
ment. He figured, rightfully so, that I'd choose to send
you off again. And being strong-willed, that you might
again choose your own destination, reasonably back
to your car. Don't forget, no one knew your car was
back in Orlando. That really had Nelson and Harris
stumped. They just couldn't figure out where you'd
stashed the old beater!

"So after he flushed us out of the house yesterday
with the threatening message in the snow, he followed
Rex and me to the station, then just waited with the
hope that I'd flee."

"Being the spitfire that your are." Then, on a more wistful note, he added, "I just hope Gwen can muster up some fighting spirit to rebuild her dreams for a home and family."

"My heart aches for her," Joy said gently. "But she has admitted that she's better off without Harris. The monster would eventually have revealed his true colors to her and she would've been in great peril."

Dan ran a gentle thumb over Joy's bruised cheek. "Thanks for comforting her today. She's been far less than cordial to you. I appreciate your patience."

"No woman deserves to suffer at the hands of a man like Harris."

"Seeing you in your battered condition graphically showed her his dark side. Harris was smooth, you know. Kept her content for eighteen months. Controlled himself because of her social connections, I figure."

"She'll have to learn to trust again. To love again."

Dan nodded. "We'll help."

"So, will Mrs. Nettel ever forgive us for suspecting her?" Joy wondered aloud, tracing her finger in the curve of Dan's ear.

"Done and done," Dan assured, wrinkling his nose over her tickling touch. "The poor thing's only goal was to reward me for bringing her no-account brother to justice. She changed her last name to avoid the negative publicity after the trial. And to help me incognito. She really does consider me a surrogate son."

"I suppose you didn't think to ask her about the TV producer with the children's program," Joy guessed.

"I did that a little while ago when I dashed next door with a bottle of wine. My motives were completely selfish," he admitted over her delighted murmurs. "If I can get you out of those smoky clubs and into a day-time job, I'll have you to myself at night. She called him on the spot. You have an appointment tomorrow at two."

"Oh, I love you so much, copper!"

Dan raked a hand through her tide of hair. "And I you, honey."

"What are we going to call her from now on?" Joy wondered aloud. "Shirley Nelson. Shirley Nettel/Nelson. What?"

Dan flashed her an impatient look. "Only you would wonder. I promise we'll ask her soon. Which reminds me," he said abruptly. "Rex doesn't want you calling him Rex Velvet, or Velvet Man, or anything like that. He's worked hard to conceal his past, make a go of it as a policeman."

"Bunch of spoilsports." She pouted, staring off into space. "It's a comedienne's mission to twist words, embellish characters of fact and fiction."

Shifting slightly, he drew Joy onto his lap. "You'll have plenty to focus your energies on in the near future. Like getting married. Having a peck of kids. Hopefully leading a relatively sane life."

"Sounds divine," Joy rejoiced, squeezing him tight. "I can't wait to name all those little Burkes."

"Whoa!" Dan protested. "Your obsession with names makes you a loose cannon. I think it best that I name our children."

"Alone?" she demanded bleakly, squeezing his shoulder blades. "Without consulting me?"

"I don't care much for those snazzy show-biz zingers of yours, all starting with twin letters, like Constance Clarence, Esther Emerson and Faye Fairway. I can't live with a Buddy Burke, a Bygolly Burke, Beany Burke, Babycakes Burke."

"Well," she huffed, "I suppose you don't care for Joy Jones when it comes right down to it!"

"Nonsense, honey," he crooned, stroking her tousled hair. "I love it. It's you."

"It is my true and legal name, you know," she hastened to assure him.

Dan's blue eyes were solemn. "Of course, it is."

"Though," she trailed off merrily, "it is a rather recent name."

"What!"

"That's right," Joy affirmed, closing his sagging jaw with a clack. "I changed it several years ago when I started doing comedy." She laughed at his dumbfounded expression. "Didn't you even suspect?"

"Guess not," he admitted. "You're so damn distracting."

"Good," she purred, kicking away the afghan. "Sounds like the perfect edge for a long-besotted union."

"What is your birth name?" Dan asked casually.

"You're the detective, Danny," she retorted airily. "So detect."

"I believe I'll take the easy way out," he threatened with mock gruffness. "Grill the whole truth out of you with my bare hands. Make you talk."

Joy lifted a golden brow, aware of the roughened fingertips already creeping up beneath her sweatshirt. "Think it'll work?"

"I have my ways, baby. Gotta warn ya, though, it might take all night."

Joy's green eyes twinkled. "Then by all means, copper," she purred. "Make me."

Look out for Temptation's bright, new, stylish covers...

They're Terrifically Tempting!

We're sure you'll love the new raspberry-coloured Temptation books—our brand new look from December.

Temptation romances are still as passionate and fun-loving as ever and they're on sale now!

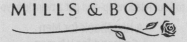

MILLS & BOON

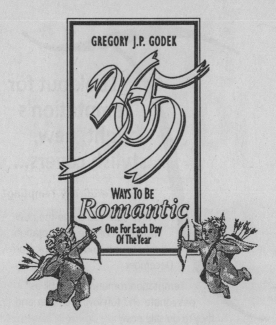
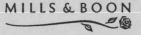

PENNY JORDAN

❦

Cruel Legacy

One man's untimely death deprives a wife of her husband, robs a man of his job and offers someone else the chance of a lifetime...

Suicide — the only way out for Andrew Ryecart, facing crippling debt. An end to his troubles, but for those he leaves behind the problems are just beginning, as the repercussions of this most desperate of acts reach out and touch the lives of six different people — changing them forever.

Special large-format paperback edition

OCTOBER   **£8.99**

W❂RLDWIDE

This month's irresistible novels from

Temptation

WILD LIKE THE WIND by Janice Kaiser

Fire, Wind, Earth, Water—but nothing is more elemental than passion.

Julia Powell believed she could live without passion. But she couldn't survive without her abducted daughter, Zara. She was willing to do whatever it took to get her back, including marrying a man she hardly knew—the notorious Cole Bonner...

JOYRIDE by Leandra Logan

Dan Burke was not looking forward to Christmas...until Joy Jones arrived on his doorstep, needing help. A second chance with Joy was what he had secretly dreamed of, but could Dan survive having his heart broken again?

JUST HER LUCK by Gina Wilkins

It was just Andie McBride's luck to be tracked down by a sinfully sexy man sent by her suffocating family. He might turn her into a mass of quivering desire, but he, too, was domineering. Had her luck run out?

I'LL BE SEEING YOU by Kristine Rolofson

After fifty years, destiny brought two wartime lovers back together. Destiny also brought Nicholas Ciminero and Sarah McGrath together, and it was as if they were made for each other. But were they destined to repeat the mistakes of the past?

Spoil yourself next month
with these four novels from

AFTERSHOCK by Lynn Michaels

Fire, Wind, Earth, Water—but nothing is more elemental than passion.

Rockie Wexler's father had disappeared, and she needed some help rescuing him. It came in the shape of Leslie Sheridan—but didn't he have reasons for hating the Wexler name?

LOVE POTION No. 9 by Kate Hoffmann

When Susannah invented a love potion, it seemed to work: handsome Jay Beaumont fell in love with her. But she'd never intended to fall in love with him…

ANGEL OF DESIRE by JoAnn Ross

Dreamscape Romance

Rachel Parrish had to stop Shade's quest for vengeance. But she hadn't counted on her very *womanly* response to him. Because Rachel had been heaven-sent with no experience of earthly pleasures…

LOVERBOY by Vicki Lewis Thompson

Luke Bannister, TV's sexiest star, was finally coming home. But childhood sweetheart Meg wasn't going to join his harem. He had dumped her once—she wasn't about to let it happen again!